Corn Maiden

by

JOYCE JONES

Lean
Press

Portland, Oregon

Editor: Mary Junewick, Portland, Oregon

Cover design and original artwork by Stephen S. Scates, Graphiquorum Design Services, Portland, Oregon

Composition and page design by William H. Brunson, Typography Services, Portland, Oregon

Printed by Malloy Lithographers, United States

ISBN: 1-932475-00-1

Lean Press
www.leanpress.com
1-503-708-4415

05 04 03   2 3 4

Hey

Lean to hear my feeble voice

At the center of the sacred hoop.

You have said that I should make the tree to bloom.

With tears running Oh Great Spirit, my Grandfather

With running eyes, I must say the tree has never bloomed

Here I stand, and the tree is withered

Again I recall the great vision you gave me.

It may be that some little root of the sacred tree still lives.

Nourish it then that it may leaf and bloom and fill with singing birds!

Hear me, that the people may once again find the good road and the shielding tree.

Black Elk
EARTH PRAYERS

PROLOGUE

In the lifetime of the teller this happened. A young man of our
people, the Boy Who Rode Sharks, was fishing one day in the boat
he had carved himself from the spirit of the cedar, when Thunderbird,
spirit of the storm, spread his great wings and raised a gale. The young
man was helpless in the spirit storm. He was washed up half dead on
the shore of the Spirit World. When he had recovered, the storm was
gone and it was dark.

The Boy Who Rode Sharks saw a bright light coming toward
him across the water. He watched as the tide brought it within reach.
It was a fine cedar tree, glowing brightly. He helped it up onto the
beach. The light was so bright that the young man had to turn his
head away. When he looked at it again, a beautiful woman lay on the
sand where the tree had been. There was kelp in her long, cedar-
colored hair. The Boy Who Rode Sharks was amazed, but he built a
fire to warm and dry the woman.

Together they sat on the sand before the fire and watched the
moon on its long journey across the sky. Finally, the Boy Who Rode
Sharks could bear the weight of his curiosity no longer.

"Who are you?" he asked.

She did not duck her head and stare at the sand like the women
he knew. Instead, she turned the full glow of her moon-filled eyes
upon his face. She answered slowly, in his own tongue.

"I am one of the people who serve the Corn Goddess. Our
mother is the earth and our father the sun. I was born of the sun's

radiance and the earth's tears. My roots are in the earth and I grow and change with the seasons. I sow my seeds and nourish them and care for the young plants. When they produce seeds of their own, I harvest them and begin again. Such is my life. I will never die so long as the cycle is completed. When I am harvested, my own flesh will be sown in mounds of earth, with the corn and the bean and the squash seed, to nourish the bursting grain. Then as the new growth pushes up through the earth into the sunlight I shall live again. It is promised."

The Boy Who Rode Sharks did not understand her. Her words were strange to his ear. "How do you come to be here, floating on the tide like a cedar log?" he asked.

The woman hid her face in her long hair and wept quietly for a time before she answered. "I angered my people. I was chosen to be Corn Maiden and I refused the honor. I refused to spread the pollen, which brings a return of the crop, and to bestow the blessing on the sprouting seed, which renews life and hope to our people. Without the crop there would be no food. It was a terrible disgrace to my family."

"Your words are foreign to me," The Boy Who Rode Sharks said. "I do not understand 'crop' or 'corn.' Why did your family not hunt and fish for their food as my people do?"

The woman nodded. "It is told that when the world was very new, my people, too, hunted and fished for their food and traveled from place to place following the game," the woman said. "Then there came a time when the sun grew angry and parched the earth. The game deserted us and food was difficult to find. When we were desperate, Thunderbird came to us bringing with him the seeds of a new life. We stopped traveling and planted the seeds.

"Thunderbird brought rain to nourish the plants. When we harvested the food, we built a new dwelling place in which to keep it during our time of rest, until we should plant the seeds again. We learned a new way of living, with new gods and new rituals, and lived in peace and harmony with the earth, the sun, and with each other. We are the Corn Goddess's chosen people and shape our lives in her image. Each year a young woman is chosen from among us to become the Corn Maiden to serve the Corn Goddess, to ensure that the corn will grow again."

"Why would you not accept the honor your people gave to you? Why would you not become Corn Maiden?"

The woman gazed into the fire for a long time before she answered him. Then she shaped her words carefully. "I had a vision in which the Spirit Changing Woman told me I was to become the mother of a new people. But the Corn Maiden must become a bearer of children and carrier of water, a tender of plants and other young growing things. I have seen my mother and the other women worn with such bearing and carrying and tending, bending lower and lower until they touch the earth from which they came, and reenter it. Their bodies continue to serve the young. Changing Woman had said that I had other services to perform. I was not ready to become a slave of the corn."

"But how did you come here?"

"My people in their anger wished to sacrifice me to the sun. But the sun in his great wisdom took pity on me and the vision I had received and told Thunderbird to carry me away on the wind. A great sandstorm carried me for many suns and many moons far over the desert, past the mountain gods, until I came to a vast forest of enormous trees of a variety I had never seen before. I was rooted there among them, beside a stream, and found that I had become a tree.

"It was quiet and peaceful there but I grew tired of always standing alone and I felt time passing. Then one night I felt an excitement in the air and knew my time had come. The sun had not forgotten my vision. There was a windstorm, the twin of the one that brought me there. The mountain gods threw fire and lightning bolts at one another. I was new and my roots were shallow. I fell with a jolting crash into the stream that rose up and carried me down to the wide, swift river. After many turnings I came into the sea and floated through many tide changes until I was cast upon this shore at your feet." Shyly she looked up at the young man through her long, wet hair.

The Boy Who Rode Sharks looked at the woman in wonder.

"You are most beautiful," he said. "Are you warmed now after your long journey in the sea? Are you ready to become my Corn Maiden?"

"I am tired of standing alone," she said.

ONE

I am being tracked like an animal. Queen Anne Hill and the safety and comfort of my former life are behind me, cut off by my pursuer. Unfamiliar city blocks of fear stretch out before me. I know now how the deer, innocent victim, grass eater, killer of nothing, feels at the scent of a predator. I, too, am prey. I move away slowly. The dark, raincoated figure with the dog follows.

He has followed me since I left the coffee shop. Awareness of his presence has nagged me for blocks. I thought at first it could be a coincidence. He could just be out walking his dog. But I stopped. He stopped. I took a short cut. He followed. I doubled back a block and now I am sure.

He stands at the end of the street, preventing my retreat back up the hill to safety. In his right hand he holds a stick like a club; slowly, deliberately, he slaps his left palm with it. The dog sits, watchful, at his feet. It is a large dog, a German Shepherd, its very breed a menace.

Confused by this open threat, I pretend to be checking an address from my purse. I convince no one. What do I do now? This cannot be happening. It is unreal. I need a plan. I must not give in to panic. Keep a normal pace. Stay in the open, away from dark corners where he would be able to make his move. And above all, try not to think about what that move might be.

I am lost. I am walking through a maze of small factories and warehouses that I would normally drive past. Today, nothing is normal.

It is my birthday and I have decided to walk. How far does this forsaken part of town reach? How many blocks before I find traffic and stores and people? Six, eight blocks? That's a long way. Not far if I was driving. If only I had taken the car. But I wanted to face the day unfettered. Now I long for my car's protection.

Where is everyone? There is no movement anywhere, no cars in the large parking lots. The gates to the factories are locked. Of course, it is Saturday, not a working day. No wonder the area is deserted. It is ironic. It is ridiculous. The sun shines wanly. The wind cuts with an icy edge. The morning is cleanly carved out of a golden block of normality. But I am locked into an obscene game with this unknown figure. We are hunter and hunted. I have become part of his evil plan. It is unfair. I resent this invasion of my identity.

I want to protest, to turn around and confront him. But I must not indulge the thought of confrontation. He would be forced to precipitate his action. And there is no one to interfere. I am easy prey. I have no weapons, no defenses. I am a gentle creature, like the deer. It would take little force to overcome me. I become repulsed by even the thought of violence.

I am a physical coward. I am afraid of other people's violence. I have always been. Old shame flames my face, but it is no use. My knees have lost their strength. I am weak with fear. In my mind I slip further and further down the evolutionary chain until I am a worm. Buildings and fences confine me, reducing my options. I keep moving somehow, hoping for some hole to crawl into.

The coffee shop! If only I could reach it. But it seems to have given me up to this maniac. I have fled to this shop for years for comfort, ever since the children were old enough to be left alone. It is where I go when I need someone else to wait on *me*. Will I ever see it again? A pang of loss grips me. Of all the places in my life, I miss that one the most. I long for its warmth and familiarity. So many times I have fled the pain of demands that were beyond my capacity to fulfill, to hold a cup of coffee in my hands and let the warmth of the liquid and the undemanding anonymity of the place seep into my soul until the shudders subsided and the inner screaming was still. It is my soul's home, the home of what still exists inside me, apart from the roles I play. There, I am a person who drinks coffee at the neighborhood café, half ashamed of the compulsion that makes me a regular customer there.

The house on Queen Anne Hill is not mine. It belongs to *them*. To the children and to Richard. It always will. I am merely its caretaker. I have never felt at home there. Even now that the children are grown and gone, their ghosts fill the empty rooms. And they keep coming back, popping in for a weekend, and for holidays. They think poor mummy might get lonely. I hate the holidays. I pronounce myself finally and eagerly separated from motherhood. As of today, this birthday, the children are no longer my responsibility. Today, my life is supposed to begin. But now, in a matter of minutes, it may end.

Right now I would trade my hard won freedom for the sight of a familiar face. I have never felt so isolated. If the children had been with me, nothing like this would have happened. I would have taken the car. The closeness of the pack, the presence of all those bodies was a shield against terror. My concern for them and their constant demands were a distraction that kept the wolves of my imagination at bay. At least during the daylight. I have never been so alone, and so unprotected. There is no one here to distract me. And the hunter is closing in from behind.

There is a horrible familiarity about this present nightmare. In the early hours of this morning I had the dream again. It is always the same dream. A tiger stalks. He is in the next room stalking the children and me. He is too close. The walls seem as fragile as paper. I can hear his hoarse breath. There is no door I can close, just an opening through which he will come at any moment.

Quickly, quietly, the children and I move into another room. He is coming. I can hear the clicking of his claws on the wooden floor. He will catch us in a moment. I know how the dream will end. Just as it always does. He will attack the children and begin to rip them apart, his fangs dripping blood, tearing flesh, dismembering tiny limbs. The children's screams will rend me. And I will stand there helpless. I can never make the move that a mother should make to stop the slaughter, to throw myself upon the animal to distract him, to sacrifice myself for the children. Instead I will run. I always run. I do not need to finish the dream. I cannot finish it anymore. I wake up before the ending, rigid with terror, drenched with guilt.

I do not understand. That dream belongs to the past, to all the years I was trapped in a house with four small children. Today was to have been my first day of freedom. I am leaving the old nightmare for a new one, a walking horror. Is this what freedom is like? To walk in fear? Or do I feel defenseless because of my sheltered life? I have always been wrapped in male protection, first my father's, then my husband's. I chafed at the restrictions, I longed to be free of them, to risk the threat of exposure to the outside world. And now I am alone and the wind is cold. I shiver and keep moving.

I want to go back, to reverse the film. I have always imagined that I could do that with the power of my mind if I wished it intensely enough. I want to replay that which has happened and change the pattern. Is this the time? Do I need it badly enough?

A lone car is parked by the curb ahead of me. I formulate and reject plans to use it to escape. I look in casually as I walk past. There are no keys in the ignition. The window lock button looks depressed. I resist the temptation to try the door handle. If it were unlocked, I would not dare lock myself inside. He would have me trapped. And if it were locked, as it seems to be, he will know that I am panicking. I walk on, trying not to notice my reflected image in the car window. The attractive figure is satisfying but today I am regretting its slenderness, its unmistakable femininity. The blurred white face with staring eyes I do not recognize. It is the face of panic. I hurry past it.

Where is my husband? Richard, of course, is out of town. Richard has never been available when I have a problem. He arranges it. Richard dislikes problems. We have been married for twenty-two years, and I have had the nightmare about the tiger perhaps once or twice a year for at least the first fifteen of those years. I have never told Richard about it. It is not the kind of thing you tell Richard; there would not be anything he could do about it. You tell Richard when the car is knocking, or the furnace needs repair, or when one of the children needs an orthodontist. Those are the kinds of things that Richard can handle, something he can fix. Usually with money. I would not tell him that I am afraid that my life is draining away, that I can feel it going. "Nonsense," Richard would say. "You've been watching too much TV."

Poor Richard. The police will make him identify the body. That thought almost makes dying worthwhile. Almost. I wonder if I will be recognizable. It would be like Richard to deny that it is me. To deny it all.

Why is there no traffic? No lovely cruising patrol car, checking on all the empty parking lots, the padlocked gates? No one. It is hopeless. I keep walking down the hill, toward the Sound, as fast as I dare, hoping for some opportunity to escape. There seems to be none. I am trapped. The man and dog are close behind me now. I hate being trapped. I did twenty-two years of motherhood. I never for a moment thought about running away, deserting my responsibilities. Which was a miracle, considering. Nor did I think about working during those years. I had too much guilt and not enough energy. Four kids is a full-time job. I stayed. And I did my time.

Running has always been my primal response to tension. Whenever I have a problem, my first instinct is to flee. To walk, to run, to drive, anything to get away. I exorcise my pain with movement. I started walking when I was eight or nine in Iowa, to escape the sound of my father's bullying and my mother's defensive whine. When I was eleven, we moved to South Texas. away from the plains' winters. We lived in a fifteen-by-twenty-foot shack, my father, my mother, my sister, and I, in the middle of the desert. It was two miles to the nearest town and a mile to the nearest neighbor. The four of us shared the same tiny space and nothing else. Each of us was as isolated as the house. I spent as much time as possible outside, walking for hours after school and on weekends when the school was closed, walking though the dusty fields, totally alone. I dreaded holidays then, too, for different reasons. Flight had magical, soothing powers. I was never lonely then. I talked to myself. I read voraciously, mostly about the past. And in the silence I learned to listen.

And then I sentenced myself for life to four children, to never being able to move without them, and the constant pressure of their demands and their noise. At last that is over. I deserve time off for good behavior. I was to have regained my mobility today. Now it seems I am going to lose it forever.

Where is he? Is he still there? How close? I can not resist; I have to look. I angle across the street, looking casually for nonexistent traffic. He is much closer. He sees me looking at him. He catches my eyes, and pulls out a pair of gloves. Slowly, efficiently, he puts them on. I finally wrench my eyes away. What does he mean to do? Strangle me, I suppose. They do that often in sex crimes. Bare hands can leave identifiable prints.

Something has been fooling around with perspectives. Time has slowed to nothing. Every footstep takes an eternity. Distances have become enormous. Buildings blot out the sky. I am so tired. Every step is an effort. I breathe heavily. My arms are dead weights, my legs seem somehow to be moving, though I can no longer feel them. Perhaps when the end comes, I shall sink into it like sleep and not feel anything. I do not believe that.

Images sort through my mind like late night news clips. They are all fears. I did not know I had so many. It seems that my whole life has been filtered through a screen of my fears. I find that I have total recall of every gory newspaper story I have ever read; sex crimes, murders, and rapes flash through my mind in lurid detail like a police file. But I have never seen pictures of these things before, I am sure. It seems curious, but there they are, the printed stories translated into pictures for storage in my brain cells. All the movies that ever frightened me as a child are there, all the horror stories I was told, and nightmares I have known and lost. People I feared, large fears, small fears, a terrifying collection. There seems to be no end. My life has had no safe harbors, only temporary footholds between abysses of terror. The images run together into one horrible impression. Out of it an occasional picture comes floating to the surface. One such long-lost image bobs into nauseatingly close focus.

I am four again. My father, whom I adored as a god, is holding me out over the railing of a bridge. He is pointing out something in the river below, something he wants me to remember. I am too terrified to even know what it is I am supposed to see. I can only concentrate on the distance of the fall, the amount of thin air below me. My father would never have let me fall. From the perspective of time I know he would have jumped in himself rather than risk dropping me. But at that moment I can only doubt. I distrusted him for the first time. For a moment I feared that he might be going to deliberately throw me into the river below. The image of the gray, coarse-textured cement bridge railing with its decoration of pigeon droppings is permanently stamped on my consciousness as a symbol of security. If only I could grasp it with both hands right now, throw myself upon it and wrap my arms and legs around its bulk, I might survive. Ultimately, my father realized how nervous I was (I would not cry out in front of him), and he put me down onto the concrete. My legs were rubbery with relief. If only I could recapture that feeling of disaster avoided.

This is so unfair. My life has never had a chance. And now I may die. I have postponed living until it is too late. There are so many things left undone, places unseen, things unlearned, people not met, stories untold. All anticipation is reduced now to a mad hope that my stalker will not drag my death out. If I am to die, please let it be swiftly. I am terrified of pain. I do not want to know that it is happening. Please God, not the dog! That would be too slow. Rather a knife, a gun, a club, anything to speed up oblivion and release. He is getting closer. I feel a scream rising in my throat. I am losing the last fragments of control.

I am so preoccupied with my fear that I do not fully understand what is happening. I see, but do not comprehend, a man ahead of me walk out of a factory gate and cross to a motorcycle parked at the curb. He turns to look at me. For a moment I add him to my nightmare. He is blocking my escape from the man behind me. But he adjusts his helmet, starts his engine, and takes off down the street before I realize that he might have been able to save me, to stop the coming slaughter. I stand there, tears running down my face, helpless with disappointment. I do not know how long I stand there waiting. But it must be the length of time it takes the man on the motorcycle to circle the block. He is back, pulling up at the curb beside me.

"Can I help? Want a lift somewhere?"

I reach out my hand, unable to speak. He smiles, very gently, reassuringly, and gestures to the back of the machine. Somehow I get on, my tight, suit skirt above my knees. I have never ridden on a motorcycle before.

"Put your arms around my waist," he directs. I do not need urging. I am clinging to him like the drowning woman that I am. Only then do I have the courage to look up. My pursuer and his dog are standing frozen, not six feet away. They must have been standing there for some time. The cyclist yells at them as he swings back into the street.

"Go home, George. Fun's over for today!" The raincoated figure salutes as he watches us ride away.

A new fear clutches me. He knows the man. Are they in league then? Was the first man just setting me up for another horror? Have I fallen for a terrible plot? The cyclist seems to sense my distrust. He stops at the corner and half turns.

"You're going to have to loosen up a little or you're going to tip us over. This is like riding a bicycle. You have to move with it, okay? I'm sorry old George scared you."

"You know him?" I manage to choke out the words through clenched teeth. I have not loosened my hold on him.

"I've seen him around. Or rather, her. George is really a woman. A real bull dike. She hangs out in the taverns around here. Everybody in the neighborhood knows about her. That's all she ever does, follow women to scare the shit out of them. That's how she gets her kicks. She's satisfied. She'd never do anything to you. It's safe now. You can get off here if you want to, or I can drop you at a bus stop or someplace."

I hang on tighter. "I don't think I could walk just yet," I say with difficulty. My mouth is too dry for my tongue to work properly. I must sound pretty pathetic. The biker rides on. I cling to his broad wool-shirted back as though it were a concrete bridge railing. I do not dare believe it is over, but I am too weak to care.

TWO

The biker is heading back the way I have come. In a few short blocks (it seemed so much further!) he pulls into the parking lot of the coffee shop that I left a lifetime ago, or was it only an hour ago? How could he know to bring me here?

My need to get inside the shop is pathetic, but my body refuses to cooperate. I have to be helped off the bike like an invalid. I would feel embarrassed, but it takes all my concentration to learn to walk on my unfamiliar legs.

Once inside the heavy wooden door I am safe. The hostile world is shut outside. My favorite booth is empty. I sink into it gratefully. With some hesitation, my rescuer sits opposite me.

"Thank you." The words seem so inadequate.

"Any time."

"For everything," I continue. "For rescuing me and especially for bringing me here. How did you know?"

He smiles. "I've had lunch here a couple of times myself when I was working at Simonson's, back where I found you."

"I don't remember ever seeing you, but I'm rarely here at lunch time. I am infinitely grateful."

Nancy, who waited on me earlier, fills our coffee cups, curiously, but we do not enlighten her. This is not easy to explain. I do not understand it myself. I lift my cup with both hands and sip once again as its comfort works the usual magic on my nervous system. I feel relief stemming the flow of adrenaline. It is finally over.

"Better?" He asks, watching me.

"Much. I'll recover."

"Good. I'll finish my coffee and leave you in peace."

"Oh. Please don't go! Really. Unless you're in a hurry? Unless you have somewhere you have to be?"

He smiles. "I do, but you are more important."

"Thank you. I need help. To assimilate what happened. None of this morning has been real."

"I guess George is hard to take."

"Who? Why? How?"

"George? Who knows what makes George do the things she does or what strange convolutions formed her? All I know is, she has a veteran's pension. I assume that was the WACS way of dismissing the problem. Mental disability I would imagine. Beyond that, nothing. She and Marybeth, the dog, spend a lot of time and effort perfecting their hunting techniques. They must have had insomnia today because they generally operate at night. I guess they'll sleep well enough now."

"How do you know that much?"

"Talk at the plant. The guys I worked with used to hang out at the taverns she frequents. I haven't been back here for a couple of years, but George doesn't seem to have changed much."

I squirm with disgust. I am their latest victim! I resent being victimized! How dare they involve me in their sordid perversions!

"I feel like I've been raped!"

"Of course. It was sexual aggression. You were used in a sick fantasy."

"Somebody should put a stop to it! Doesn't anybody ever complain?"

"I suppose most victims are relieved to be let off with no worse than a scare. George has been picked up on suspicion a couple of times, but there's not much the police can do, because George never actually does anything."

"It's degrading. I'm ashamed."

"Why? It wasn't your fault."

13

"I'm ashamed because I was such a coward. I let it happen! I didn't stand up to him! To her! I should have fought back, done something in my own defense! I feel like some kind of worm."

"It's not cowardly to fear for your life. You had reason to believe George's threat was real. Cowards are little people. I think you are not small inside. You just haven't found your full courage yet."

He is sincere. How can he know I need to hear this! I answer him.

"I wish I had another chance! I know that's easy to say once it's over, but next time I won't be such an easy mark. I'm mad now. If I have to go, at least I'll go down fighting."

"I believe you. You have hit bottom. That's where everybody's courage starts. Anger is a sign of recovery. I can take you home now. Unless you'd rather stay here?"

"Oh no! I can't go home. It's my birthday!" My response startles us both.

Nancy refills our coffee cups. We wait politely for her to leave.

"Happy birthday," he says, raising his cup in a mock toast.

"Thank you. So far it's been amazing!" My laugh is shaky. "But to go home now would be to admit defeat. Besides, this is my real home." I gesture around the room. "My real life is here. I only *exist* in the house up on the hill."

"Why would going back to that house be admitting defeat?"

For some reason I need to explain to him, to make him understand. "For twenty years I've shut out large parts of the world, or at least my own interaction with it. Today I went out to see what was still out there. If I go running back to that house in fear, I'll admit that I can't handle it, that I can't live in the world anymore by myself. I'm not ready to admit that yet."

"Then I should leave you to rally and try again."

"No. Please?" I find myself pleading. The image of the empty house with all its bitterness and regrets and its ghostly tenants panics me. I cannot go back. "I'm not ready to leave here. I feel so exposed. You're solid ground in a world that's become a quagmire. I need to take one step at a time. It hasn't been a fair trial. I can't go back, and I'm not ready to go on yet, alone. I guess that's a terrible imposition. I have no right to ask it."

He grins. "I suppose a rescuer has to finish the job he starts. Sounds like you aren't quite rescued yet."

"Thank you, one more time. For understanding. That says a lot about you. Not every stranger is so perceptive."

I study him for the first time objectively. He is young, damned young. He is dark: skin, hair, eyes, clothing. His features are broad, but not unpleasantly so, all rough lines like a crude artist's sketch. He's rugged. A bit Asian, perhaps. He sees the assumption in my eyes. He has been watching for it.

"I'm Indian," he says defiantly.

"And I'm a forty-two-year-old female, middle-aged and scared shitless."

He laughs. "That makes us about even on the handicap scale."

"Which tribe?"

"Kloot. We've got a reservation over on the Peninsula."

"You're the first Indian I've ever met."

"And you're the first female WASP in midlife crisis I have ever talked with."

"You make me sound like an in insect on a collector's pin, but I suppose you're right. I suppose that's all that's wrong with me. Sociological labels make problems sound so trite."

"That's their purpose. They cut away all individuality. Gives some people a sense of security, being like everybody else."

"I think I prefer unique and miserable."

"If it's any consolation to you, you belong to a unique group in the history of the world. I assume your isolation from the world that you spoke of a minute ago has to do with the rearing of children? Your Western customs are unfortunate. Native American children belong to the tribe, or at least to an extended family unit, which frees the mother to contribute more actively to the welfare of the entire unit, and eliminates her isolation."

"How civilized!"

He laughs bitterly. "Yes, isn't it? In any case, you belong to the first wave of women who are physically able to rear your families and have the health and energy left to start another life. Not too many years ago you wouldn't have survived your childrearing years. And if you had, you'd have been old, and physically spent."

"I don't exactly have the energy of a twenty-year-old! How did you know I meant that I had been taking care of children? I might have been a spinster looking after my aging parents, or a religious recluse."

His glance is warm. "Impossible," he says. "You may feel unfulfilled, but you don't look unused. You look like a complete woman, useful, used, but not used up."

"Secondhand Rose. I certainly feel used up. Sometimes that house was so full of living things I wanted to scream. Plants, animals, children, adults; all dependent on me! I read once that the female wasp lays her eggs inside a larvae, and the baby wasps eat their host when they hatch. I know how that larvae feels."

"All that's over now?"

"I hope so. Now I am about to find out if there is life after children."

"At least you have an advantage over the twenty-year-old whose energy you envied. You've already lived one lifetime. You can start the second with all the knowledge you gained from the first!"

I find myself crying quietly. Who is this young man who speaks like a psychologist and one of his own tribal legends at the same time? How can he know me better than I know myself? It is overwhelming.

"You mean all those years weren't wasted?" I am trying to keep the sobs out of my voice.

"Wasted?!!" His anger is totally unexpected. "The parable of talents, I suppose! You aren't worthwhile unless you have made a lot of money by the time you're thirty! Damned Christian superachievers! Destroying your self-worth because of some unrealistic goals. Life doesn't demand anything of you except that you survive and multiply. You did that. The rest you have to demand of yourself. What good is a culture that values the material and devalues human beings? Look at you. Materially you have more than you'll ever use. But emotionally you're starving!"

So simple. So obvious. And no one else had ever troubled to reassure me. Had cared enough. He seems to care. I don't know if it's my vulnerability that has touched him, or if he cares about all helpless creatures but I feel some kind of love and passion flowing from him. I am caught in its surge. My parched soul soaks it up greedily. I have no defense against this kind of conquest.

I have known so little sincere masculine attention. The social charade of gallant flattery is as unsatisfying as a diet pop. And Richard never notices how I look, or cares. I know how vulnerable I am. I could fall for a casual line as thoroughly as I did for George's masquerade. I believe what men tell me. I lack the hard shell of the sexually liberated woman. But then, you have to believe sometimes, to trust your instincts. Otherwise you stay alone. I do not want to stay alone.

"I'm a hungry stray," I gulp. "The world is full of us. You can't rescue us all." I want desperately for him to rescue me.

"No. But you strayed across my path. You have become part of my reality. *You* I can do something about."

"Why should you?"

His voice comes from far away to answer me. His eyes are focused inward.

"This does not appear to be a matter of choice. Your spirit and mine are not strangers."

I stammer, "This has to be a dream. How many times have I sat here in this very seat and wished that someone was sitting there where you are, someone I could say these things to, someone who would understand and care, who would say the kind of things you are saying to me and make me feel good about myself."

"And now that I am here?" His voice is stern, challenging.

"If only you were ten years older!"

"Does age mean that much to you?" I think he is laughing at me.

"Doesn't it to you?" I cannot keep the hope out of my question.

"The woman inside you is just a child, untouched."

"And that child wants this dream to continue." I am breathless with my audacity.

"Dreams last for just the space between the waves. Then reality comes crashing in." His voice is a warning.

"All the important things in life happen quickly," I answer. "It is the dull ones that stretch on forever. Time is relative. Do you suppose we could slow it down enough to live a lifetime between the waves?"

"Perhaps. You have a husband." It is not a question, but it requires an answer. How do I explain? It is difficult to open a wound that has festered untouched for twenty two years. I have never talked about it before. No one has asked. I want desperately to tell him. He is waiting. His eyes are knives cutting away my defenses, leaving me helpless before his judgment.

"Yes. For twenty-two years. He's not my husband, he's a habit!" I try an experimental laugh. It is not a success. The eyes are stern, waiting.

"Richard is another one of my children," I continue. "I had four children in four years. Those children have grown up. Richard will never grow up. I'm tired of motherhood."

My voice chokes on the sobs in my throat.

He makes his judgment. "A man who would not tell you that you are a woman worth having does not deserve you," he says. He takes my hand. "Let's get out of here."

I do not argue. I walk without help out into the weak sunlight. We get back onto his cycle in silence. He drives towards the water, away from Queen Anne Hill. I do not look back.

In a very short time we pull out onto the Alaskan Way Viaduct, an arterial which runs along the waterfront. A few blocks later, we turn into the parking lot of a warehouse on the water side of the highway. He helps me off the cycle and then points.

"Last chance. The bus to downtown stops over there by that bench."

He locks up the machine while I watch in agony, a thousand questions, a thousand objections choking my throat. I have to say something. "Do you want me to leave?"

He straightens up and looks at me. "What do you want?" He asks.

"I don't know! I'm confused. Maybe it's shock. God, you're so young!"

He stiffens perceptibly and walks away. I stand watching until he reaches the edge of the embankment. He turns and looks back.

"Are you coming with me or what?" he yells.

"Do you want me to?"

"I'm asking."

I go. It is not much of an invitation, but it is all I am going to get. I am not thinking. I am reacting. If I stopped to think I would stay put and catch a bus to someplace safe. But I have been someplace safe. And I am sick of it.

THREE

My rescuer disappears over the edge of the embankment. When I reach the place where I last saw him I find an open wooden staircase, ancient, weathered and broken in places, which leads down the cliff. He is almost at the bottom. He does not look back. I start down. Blackberry vines tear at my hose. I have to sit down to straddle a missing step and come away with a wicked splinter in my hand. There is, of course, no railing. What am I doing here? Where are we going anyway? He probably lives on the beach. This is insane.

The hill is very steep. After my ordeal I am still weak and the effort required by the hill is a lot to ask of a woman my age. I am out of condition. And lord knows what more is to come. I am too old for this sort of thing. This madness is for youngsters. But I can not remember ever having been that young. By the time I reach the bottom he is off across the railroad track leaving me to follow as best I can. While I am trying to pull out the splinter, my heel catches in the track and I fall. He is out of sight. I just sit there, fuming. Why did I come? I do not need this. What do I know about him anyway? He could be a Charles Manson type. He could end up chopping me up into little pieces and laughing. I might have been better off with George and Marybeth. Not to mention Richard. I never learn! How could I commit myself to a total stranger?! I wanted my freedom, and here I am with another man, and undoubtedly a chauvinist besides. Repeating the same old pattern, or maybe creating a new, worse one. It has to be the shock. I am not yet rational.

When I fail to follow, he comes back looking for me. At the sight of him, my internal organs do a disassociation trip and I know why I am here, though I am still not happy about it.

He shakes his head at the sight of me sitting on the railroad track. "It's a wonder you can walk at all," he says.

I just look at him.

"Carrying that load," he continues.

I hold up my purse and look at it. It is not especially heavy.

"No, I don't mean just the purse. Look at you! Those clothes, those shoes, hose, heels, tight skirt. How can you expect to move, or to breathe even? I'll bet you've got on a girdle."

"I don't need a girdle," I spit out through clenched teeth. "And my stupid heel's caught in the track."

"And I suppose you'd just sit there and wait for a train to come run over you rather than lose a shoe. Possessions, always possessions! You couldn't run away to save yourself because you're carrying the weight of all you own." He holds out his hand to help me up. I ignore him and struggle to my feet alone. He shrugs.

"You're even afraid to grab hold of me for fear it might obligate you. A little discomfort and you get reminded of your station in life and its fucking protections!" He starts walking away.

I wrench my shoe free of the track, put it on and follow him. "I'm not obligated," I yell at his back, "I'm angry! You're an insensitive sonofabitch!" What is happening to me?!

He looks back at me and grins. "And don't you forget it."

He has the most infuriating smile. It is tender and loving and self-sure, and so damnably smug, all at the same time. It unleashes a rip-tide of conflicting emotions in me. I have not felt that strongly toward anyone in more years than I dare to remember. I had forgotten that caring about a man could ache so much. It is like getting the feeling back in a foot that has gone to sleep, but all over.

I follow him across the tracks over the inevitable pile of drift-wood logs and down onto a scrap of beach that has somehow escaped the industrialization around it, like a relic buried in the attic of the large city. It must belong to the gulls and an occasional duck and presumably to drifters like my friend the cyclist with leftist opinions! It occurs to me that I do not even know his name. It has not seemed important. After all, he has not asked mine.

I find him standing in the sand looking out over the water. He is totally relaxed, at home, the sea breeze stirring his shoulder-length straight black hair, whipping the loose ends of his old navy CPO jacket. The sun is out. The scene has the quality of a Technicolor dream, with the shadowy unreality of a memory. I stand beside him, looking out over the marcelled waves on the Sound, and the crisply defined mountains beyond.

He takes my hand. His palm is hard and calloused. We walk back to the logs and sit down. Then he turns that appraising gaze on me. I stare back. He is clean, intelligent looking, and young, even younger than I originally thought. He seems sensitive about that. He has said age does not matter to him. What if he has a mother fixation? I am scared by my own daring, but I am definitely not thinking in terms of a mother–son relationship. He is vibrantly male and I am picking up all the vibrations. I worry about how I look to him. Is he having second thoughts?

"Do I pass inspection?" I ask finally, laughing nervously, hating myself for the laugh.

"I don't want you to think I do this all the time," he says. He laughs with me. Then he gets up and pulls me to my feet.

"You've got sand on your face already," he observes. "A definite improvement." We walk down the beach holding hands.

Skirting the waves' edge, we skip just out of reach of the water like giant sandpipers.

Watching me he asks suddenly, "Ever been swimming in it?"

I have a small chill of fright. "Never. It's cold. I'm afraid of water."

"Nonsense. It's man's second element. The Sound stays the same temperature the year around, varying maybe two degrees winter and summer. It's the air that gets cold, not the water. Fear is a giant weight around your neck." He stoops suddenly, before I realize what he is doing, he scoops me up and splashes out into the water. I want to be picked up and held, but not for this. I cling to him desperately, but he is as powerful as the current, as irresistible as the crashing waves. He wrenches me free and flings me into the water.

He neglected to mention that the unvarying temperature of the water is 40 to 42 degrees Fahrenheit, which is an icy shock to the human body with a normal temperature of 98.6. I come up choking, the air knocked out of me by the shock. The water is shallow enough so I can get my feet under me. He is standing nearby, laughing. "I baptize thee in the name of the Great Spirit," he yells.

"You crazy sonofabitch!" I wail. I hate him. I am fearfully cold, and abused, having been thrown against my will, despite my fears, into the goddamned ocean. I am furious. I struggle up and am knocked back down by a tiny wave and dragged in its backwash. I sit there and cry. Struggling no longer matters because I am already soaked. The tears feel warm on my face. I am feeling very sorry for myself, sitting there in the ocean I have looked at so long through the safety of my window at the top of the hill. I no longer need to be afraid of getting wet. I am in it up to my shoulders and I am not afraid. A feeling of release washes over me.

"This is it," I say to myself. "Here I am; I'm in it and I don't mind. I'm glad it's done. It's cold but I'll live. I'm really alive, and beginning to feel pretty good about the whole thing." I look up at the man standing and laughing at me, and I am not mad any longer. He has done this to me deliberately, because he knew that I needed it. He is not one to do things slowly, in stages; first bare feet, then bathing suits. Not this fellow.

Sitting there I begin to laugh, too. I stand up. It is colder out of the water, so I sit back down and splash around.

He has stopped laughing. "All right, that's enough," he says. "Come on out of there before you get pneumonia. I can't fuck a sick woman."

I sober up fast. He has said it! It sounds hard and deliberate. I head for shore. Once I stand up I have to move fast. It is cold.

I have never known such cold. He takes my hands and pulls me out of the water. I have lost both shoes, but I have a death grip on my dripping purse. He drags me unmercifully along the beach. My nylon-covered feet hurt on the rocks. I am shivering so hard I cannot run. His haste is as desperate as mine. I am crying and shaking and dripping. I cannot breath. I am beyond cold to trauma.

He pulls me up under the bank among the logs into a rough drift-wood lean-to I had not noticed. It is one of those structures you find on isolated beaches, not meant for serious habitation, built with great effort and ingenuity out of driftwood, just for the hell of it by some frustrated modern pioneer with an afternoon to kill. It is a poor shelter, dark, cluttered, and cold, but it is out of the wind. Light filters through wide gaps between the pieces of driftwood.

He takes off my soaked coat and blouse, wrapping me in his dry jacket and then lights a hasty fire among the charred logs of a simple fire pit. The meager heat does not begin to penetrate the depths of my arctic chill. I hover over the growing flame, still shaking uncontrollably. He is watching me intently.

"Thermal shock," he diagnoses finally. "Shit." He peels off his T-shirt. He has to help me remove the rest of my wet clothes. My fingers no longer function. He helps me pull the T-shirt over my head, and pulls me down onto his lap, wrapping his jacket around us both. His hands are rubbing me gently all over, trying to get some circulation going. His eyes search the dim interior, and light upon a rusty can propped between two logs. He deserts me momentarily to carry the can outside. I hear him scraping around on the roof, and he comes back in a moment, triumphantly.

"Rainwater," he says, putting the can on the fire. "You need something hot to drink."

I nod with difficulty. He resumes his massage. By the time the water boils, his efforts are beginning to have an effect. I am no longer shivering constantly, only spasmodically. Using a stick and his wet sleeve, he maneuvers the can out of the flame and onto the cold sand. He fishes out an old bandanna from his jacket pocket and wraps it around the can and hands it to me.

"Careful of the rim, it might be sharp, and it's damned hot," he warns. My hands are not very steady, but the warmth that has already penetrated the bandanna feels so good, I attempt to swallow some of the hot water without scalding myself. I get a mouthful down and it feels great. I am careful not to look at it. The boiling has dealt with the germs, I hope, and my need has to supercede finickiness.

"That was pretty stupid of me," he admits. "To pull a stunt like that when you've already had one shock. I should have known better."

I attempt a smile of forgiveness. I cannot speak to let him know that it is all right. His haste has impressed me. I know my body is in trouble, but I am so pleased with myself inside that I cannot get worked up about it. Besides, he is doing such a good job; I know I am in good hands. I just let him save my life. If he were drunk or cared less, I might die of exposure. Thermal shock can kill quickly. The cold water and the wind chill on my wet body have lowered my body temperature too rapidly past tolerance. In the comfort of my living room I once read about thermal shock in the Sunday Supplement. Now I am having it. It seems to me that my life is suddenly full of true life adventures. I am exhilarated by the speed at which I am traveling after all those years of barely moving. Already today my life has been in jeopardy twice and it is not yet noon! The first time was only in my imagination but I was terrified. And this time I am really in danger of dying and I am not at all afraid.

This is hardly the way I had imagined I would spend my forty-second birthday, but it augurs well for my old age. I am sitting on the sand floor of a crude lean-to on the beach, roughly naked in the arms of a young stranger. His clothing is around us both. I wonder about what is happening to my life as the warmth of his body begins to seep through from the outside and the heat of the water works from the inside until the numbness lessens and pain and cold come flooding back.

He continues to massage me gently, patiently, as I thaw. Gradually the relief of heat replaces the chill in my bones. Feeling begins to return to my body with heightened intensity. Some primitive instinct for life responds to the threat of extinction with a vengeance. I cease to be a frozen lump and become a sexually awakened female in his arms.

His hands respond to the change in my condition, becoming less therapeutic and more affectionate. "We will celebrate your return to the land of the living," he murmurs in my ear.

"How?"

"It is an ancient ceremony, common to your ancestors as well as mine, a powerful magic which joins our spirits so that hereafter we cast only one shadow."

I cling to him helpless with tenderness and need, my surrender complete. He begins to croon to my body, an ancient song without words, but a song of obvious meaning, of conquest, and of love. Apologies of the used condition of my body rise to my lips and freeze there unsaid, unnecessary. His fingers stroke the ribbed flesh of my stretch marks, gently, his song not wavering. A moment later his lips caress them, his hands trace the long waist, and the pelvic cradle, approvingly. Suddenly, for the first time, I am proud of my body, of its functional, classic lines, perfectly designed for a man's pleasure and the carrying of his children.

I become greedy, frantically impatient with his deliberate, almost ceremonial approach. His entrance is sure and triumphant. Then I am free of my body, seeing with my eyes closed, feeling with all my senses the taut bow of his body, drawn over me. There is nothing awkward or tentative about his powerful thrust, the graceful line of his back and haunches. He is the essence of sexuality, bent in an act of worship. He is life renewing itself. I want to cry with the beauty of it. Instead, I find myself drawn down, slipping wholly into pleasure, reveling in it, wallowing in it, tossed and teased through its course until I lie spent on the sand.

FOUR

I lie becalmed, remembering how it feels to be intimate with a stranger. It has been over twenty years since a lover was new, uncharted, promising. This sensation has a delicate freshness as though the long-buried memories never happened and this time is the first. A virgin by default of memory!

This particular stranger may not be the first, but he is unquestionably the best. A woman never forgets her most memorable orgasms. She can tell you where, when, who, and under what conditions. And there was only one experience in my lifetime to compare with this one. It was with Richard, eighteen years ago in a cheap motel room in Wheeling, West Virginia. We were on our way home from showing my parents their new granddaughter, our second. It was a fluke in its intensity, never repeated. And this latest one was better by several lengths.

It is incredibly rare to come so quickly without all the regulation preliminaries. I was ready, psychologically ready. That made all the difference. Was this one a lucky accident like the one with Richard? Was it just the novelty, or my physical extremity? Or does this man really know what he is doing? I am betting a chunk of my life that he does. At least I hope that I am.

It occurs to me as he rolls off me, sated, that this might be the end. A wisp of fear twines around my vitals. Suppose sex was all he wanted of me? I have no hold on him. In spite of what he has said. That could have been a line. An all-time great line. What if I was wrong at the coffee shop, if my need read love into this passion? Suppose he is content to just leave me at the bus stop and ride away alone. I turn to look at him, panicked, and find him studying me. I freeze.

"Your clothes are still wet," he says.

I nod. "I lost my shoes in the water."

There are so many questions I have to ask, so many answers I need. Does he really understand me as he seems to? Did he throw me into the Sound because he understood that it was right for me? And why was it right? I do not fully understand that myself. How can I expect him to? I lie still as he dresses and goes out.

I lie on his jacket, waiting. If I close my eyes, I can still feel the warm weight of his body. I want to make that last as long as possible. I take a deep breath and discover that I am drenched with his scent. I sniff my skin appreciatively. He has marked me as his property. I have become so used to Richard's smell that I no longer noticed it. Or perhaps Richard has not been excited enough to produce it anymore. This man's scent is masculine, pervasive. I love it. I discover three separate layers to it. The first his own, then the distinctive odor of semen, and lastly our mingled sweat. I am glad there is no shower. I never want to wash it off. I am fleetingly grateful for the surgical procedure after my fourth child that tied my tubes, freeing me of the threat of pregnancy. I can enjoy his body now without complications.

He is not gone long. He has brought back the cycle saddlebags that he left at the base of the cliff. He rummages around in them, producing things dubiously. Finally he tosses me an old khaki T-shirt and a pair of denim cutoffs. I get up reluctantly to put them on. The cutoffs are miles too big and have to be tied on with a piece of cord.

"You'll have to go barefoot," he says, surveying me with satisfaction. "You look positively disadvantaged."

I give the shelter a last affectionate glance. I am not normally house proud. I never seemed to develop a proper nesting instinct, but suddenly I am in sympathy with nesters. I have more of a feeling of belonging in this haphazard tumble of driftwood than in the expensive and undeniably beautiful house at the top of the hill I left behind me so many lifetimes ago. All of two or three hours! My ruined clothes I leave behind in the shelter, a skin I have sloughed off, outgrown, and I venture forth, quivering with cold and excitement toward an uncertain future.

My new lover mocks my progress over the rocks on city-soft soles, then hefts me easily over one shoulder, the saddlebags over the other, and walks without effort to the stairway leading up the cliff.

Carrying a woman is a primitive sexual act. I am dizzy with desire when he dumps me on the logs. I cling to him for a moment, weakly. He hugs me with his free arm, reading with instinctive male accuracy my dilemma, and chuckling. "Greedy," he says not unkindly, "That's all you get. Come on, up you go."

Fear that he means it literally rises to tighten my throat, and sudden shame. I scramble up the stairs blindly, and limp across the railroad tracks, ignoring the pain of the sharp rocks bedding the tracks. I cannot bear the risk of his lifting me again. I would cry. Perhaps I am just one more in a string of women he has taken to that shack. Maybe he built it for that purpose. How stupid I am not to have thought of it before. How naïve. Handy. I am burning, suddenly sure that I have been imagining that he cares for me, sure that he will leave me at the top of the hill. I have been so easy, so eager. For crissakes, I still do not even know his name!

He is behind me all the way up the hill and across the parking lot. I hesitate as I reach the motorcycle. Perhaps I should keep going and not give him the satisfaction of brushing me off. But I am not exactly dressed for bus riding and I decide I would rather make it difficult for him. Besides if I am wrong . . . if he does want me along . . . he might misunderstand and think I do not want to go with him. I practice a cool, tough grin, one that could handle a casual, "So long, kid, see you around." But even I can tell it fails to come off.

He is fastening the bags back on the cycle, ignoring me. Or pretending to. Could he possibly think I am having second thoughts myself? About leaving Richard and my soft life? Yes, he could. It would, in fact, be like him. What was it he said before, "I don't want you to think I do this all the time!" He did say that. I cannot just walk away.

He mounts the machine, tosses me the helmet, and waits. I catch the thing and look at it. I cannot look at him. I must be pretty pathetic. My chin wobbles dangerously and I bite my lip to keep from crying.

"If you're coming, get on the fucking bike!" he says. "We've got a lot of miles to cover."

I get on, behind him, and wipe my tears on the back of his T-shirt. I am wearing his jacket, but I no longer need it. The cold cannot touch me. I do not know where we are going or what I am letting myself in for, but he wants me to go with him. That is enough. It is insanity. I recognize the symptoms. I am madly in love.

We stop for a light and I pull on his sleeve. He half turns so I can yell in his ear.

"I love you," I yell over the roar of the motor. "What's your name?"

He guns the motor as the light changes. I can feel the laughter rise from somewhere in the root of him. At the next light, he fishes out his wallet and hands it back to me, open to his driver's license. The picture is of a dark, long-haired Native American male. I find this ridiculously amusing. It is hard to read while hanging onto the back of a bike, but I manage. His name is Johnny Champion, no middle initial. Birth date: I figure quickly that he is only seven years older than my oldest daughter. He would be a more appropriate lover for her than for me. But I will be damned if I will give him up. What are my kids going to say? Or Richard for that matter? I giggle. How shocked they will all be. To hell with them. This is my life. Finally. I should probably let them know where I am. That is, when I know myself. Richard might call out the National Guard. There is plenty of time. Let Richard sweat it out for a change. He has always known where to find me. He would never look on the back of a motorcycle behind a Native American male who is two-thirds my age. I giggle. I am giggling a lot today. More than I have in years. All in all I am rather pleased with myself.

Johnny. It seems strange to call him by name. I suppose the name fits as well as any, only I feel it is a bit ordinary for him. He is not an ordinary man. At least I do not think he is. Champion seems almost a phony name, like an actor or a boxer or a wrestler. Must be a bastardization of a Native American name. I wonder what it was before? I probably could never pronounce it.

I enthusiastically continue the investigation of my lover's official papers. Height: 5 feet 11 inches. Weight: 175. He is a powerful man, strong enough to be a wrestler. He has the loose-skinned grace and the gait of a lion, aware of the power beneath his casual swagger. I must remember to ask him if he has ever wrestled. He is definitely athletic. Hair: black, God yes. Total blackness, the absence of all color. Eyes: black. A mesmerizing blackness. Light stops at their perimeters. But they reflect warmth, they glow, they burn and smoke, and they can lie dead as ashes in turn. And I quake before their examination. I could never lie to those eyes. They pass the final judgment.

His address is New Hope Bay, the reservation. Is that where we are going? Reservations are beyond my experience. How will I fit in? Will his people accept me? I have an image of abject poverty. Must I start over at my age? I have been through the penny counting, the doing without. But it would not be so bad, without kids. The hardest part was having to deny the kids. Cooking and cleaning for Johnny? Well, why not? Beats what I have been doing. I think? Dumb, that is what it is. But when was love ever smart? I will reserve judgment. I will see. Johnny is different.

I thumb quickly through the rest of the wallet: a social security number, a couple of university ID cards, a tribal ID, an old union card, and an American Express card, a peculiar status symbol for a revolutionary.

At the next traffic light I hand the wallet back.

"What do you study?" I ask.

"Anthropology, archaeology, history. The past is the only place Indians are appreciated." The ancient bitterness recognizable in his tone silences me.

We park on Second Avenue and Johnny takes me to the army-navy store. He picks out two pairs of jeans, which I must try for fit, a couple of sweatshirts, heavy socks, T-shirts, hiking boots, and a jacket like his. It is expensive. I offer to pay.

"They're for me, after all," I say with some embarrassment.

"I can afford it," he says, looking at my damp checkbook. "Use *his* money to buy clothes for *his* woman. These are for mine."

I take a deep breath and swallow that one. No wonder he is stuck with a middle-aged woman. No young one is going to buy that brand of chauvinism. But I do not complain. I am too grateful; too pleased and excited that he is taking me along for what could be a long stay, and, yes, damned flattered to be *his* woman. I feel like his woman. I want nothing else in the world. But it is painful too. I ache from having my self-respect dependent on the whims of a stranger. I have forgotten how horrible that can be. But I feel alive. There is no question of that. I have not felt this much alive in twenty years. Maybe never.

FIVE

We ride through the ripening day, life suddenly condensed into one male and one female and their movement through space. Time has been suspended in liquid sunshine with an icy wind chaser. Warm and proud in my new clothing, I swallow huge gulps of the day with fierce joy.

We arrive at a ferry terminal. I recognize it as the small town of Edmonds, about fifteen miles from Seattle, but it is altered by my new perspective. Johnny buys one one-way and one round-trip ticket. We park the cycle and sit on the grass to wait for the ferry. I savor each bite of the afternoon, delighting in its dreamlike qualities, and its novelty. Every detail is new; the wind on my cheek, the intense blue of the sky, the rough-edged silkiness of the grass between my fingers, and, above all, the joy of touching the warm male body beside me. Speech seems an intrusion on our intimacy, on the bubble of anticipation of the coming night. I have no memory of ever feeling this close to another adult. I have always been too pre-occupied with the formal structures of human relationships. With Johnny I seem to be looking out from deep inside myself, open, warm, and safe. Our separate skins have ceased to exist. Johnny takes my hand and I look with amazement at our two hands inter-twined, his large and dark and weather roughened; mine small and white and polished.

Johnny reaches into his pocket and pulls out the ferry tickets. He tears off the return half of my ticket and hands it to me. I put it away in my purse. I remove my wedding ring and solemnly put that beside the ticket. I close my purse. Our eyes meet in confirmation of the ceremony, and we break out in spontaneous laughter. Formal weddings can be so full of bitterness and disillusionment. I cried at my wedding to Richard. There is nothing but delight in our little commitment, and I feel its depth.

"Now," Johnny says, "it's your turn. Tell me your name."

"Ruth. Do you want my husband's last name or my father's?"

"Neither. What was your mother's name?"

"Her husband's or her father's?"

"Her first name."

"Kristin."

"Ruth Kristinsdottir. That is your name then."

I am enchanted, with my new name and with the man who gave it to me.

Is this the same man who, less than an hour ago, called me his woman?

That was different, I can see that now. Johnny uses the term woman as a sexual endearment. He does know the difference. I will enjoy being his woman.

It is time to board the ferry. I have always loved ferries, from the antique one-car rafts I have taken across the Mississippi and Columbia rivers to the large ocean-going ferries to Alaska and Vancouver Island. This one is not that large. It is a Washington State Ferry, which crosses the Sound between the mainland and the eastern tip of the Peninsula. Johnny's machine is stowed on the car deck, securely fastened against accident or heavy weather. We lean over the railing on the bow to watch the water and the boat traffic.

I look back at the shore slipping away from us. Back behind those hills, behind the coves and the evergreens, lies Queen Anne Hill and everything I have known. Ahead of me lies a strange world, a frightening one. I am dreadfully old to be starting over like this, like a kid. The wind off the ocean is cold; I shiver. A cloud covers the sun and Johnny looks at me. He puts his arm around me.

"You can go back anytime you want," he reminds me.

I shake my head. I am committed. But I am still uneasy. Solid earth is no longer beneath my feet. I have no idea of what lies at the other end of this journey. I am in the same position as the immigrants, my pioneer ancestors, going off into the unknown and hoping for the best. Hope. I put my arm around Johnny. Already his warmth is familiar, comforting. I have a good guide for the wilderness, the best.

Slowly my unrest begins to subside. I return to the warmth and joy of a few moments before. I relax, and enjoy my freedom, this moment between two different lives. I trust Johnny and I love him.

Johnny's closeness and the heat of the sun slowly warm and reassure me. The icy blast of sea breeze is intermittent, like the sun. It is a game the two are playing—the sun caressing my skin, smoothing down the bumps raised by the wind, dazzling the water, and then the wind dancing in to break the waves into sequined fragments, cooling the sun's heat and dashing off to give the sun its turn again.

I take deep lungfuls of the healing air. It is intoxicating. I stretch and feel my whole body sigh with contentment. I feel better than I have felt for a long time. This is a good thing that I am doing for myself. I have needed to do it for a very long time. I can feel old aches, and old soreness easing as I stretch again, as though after a long confinement.

I was a good wife, a good mother. I took care of my family. Now it is time to take care of me. Johnny feels right. In him I sense a depth beyond my own; intelligence, understanding, and layers of humanity as deep as the Sound itself. I must explore this new and so far unguessed-at world, ramble its beaches, swim in its depths, climb its mountains, and perhaps catch a glimpse of myself in its mountain lakes.

I am already a different person. I could not go back to being a creature in a cocoon if I chose. That part of my life is over. I ripped the silken shroud from my body when I decided to follow him. Already I have swelled, grown too big for it. My damp, new wings are still cramped and stiff but they will dry. I will soar.

I hug Johnny. Illogical tears burn my eyelids. I feel so fortunate to have him, this late love. I had almost given up hope of such delight. I will lie beneath him again tonight. My organs throb at the thought.

Johnny is not just something I want, like a new dress or pottery lessons. I *need* him. Every cell in my body needs him. He is rain on my desert; spring after my long winter; he is my Indian summer! This thought makes me laugh out loud. I have to share it with him.

Johnny shakes his head. "Terrible, terrible," he moans. "Bad jokes! For this I stole you away from the enemy?"

"Liberated me, I hope! Not carried me off like a trophy of war. You set me free," I correct him.

He raises his eyebrows. "We will see how free you are."

"I know I'm not strong at all. If I were strong I could have walked away from my old life alone. I needed a crutch to hang onto. After all, it's been a long time since I have walked alone! Twenty years for crissakes! I have to learn all over again. Muscles forget, lose their tone. Maybe one day I won't need that crutch. I'll make it all by myself."

He grins. "Big words. Dependence is a deep rut, a well traced pattern. Changing that after twenty years takes a lot of adaptability."

"Well, I'm here. That's the first step. The rest will follow. But I'll need your help, your support."

He shrugs. "I'm no psychiatrist. Indian males are bred as chauvinists. Where we're going you will have to pull your own weight. Both our lives could depend on it. There'll be no time to worry about whether you're free. Freedom in my world means hunger, fear, loneliness, even death. In the last extreme you can't count on anyone but yourself. It's you against the elements."

"Back to the beginning, to square one? What have I let myself in for?"

He is no longer listening. He is looking south and the tension in his body is obvious to me. Reading him is going to be easier than I thought. I am learning nonverbal communication. It requires a different level of interpersonal awareness; like wearing the same skin!

"What is it?" I ask.

"Sharks." He points but I see nothing. I look more closely, expecting dorsal fins cutting the water but see only the undisturbed water of the Sound.

"Where?"

"Keep looking," he says. "Sight down from that fishing boat about midway."

I shade my eyes against the pirouetting sunlight and stare. Finally, I see a slight disturbance, a roiling of the water and as they come closer, vague light shapes moving against the current.

"I see them! They're big! How many are there?"

"The news report said twenty. They cruised down the Sound yesterday to Olympia, and they are heading back to sea this afternoon. We're lucky to sight them."

"I thought they were only big in the movies."

"They're not that big. Six to twelve feet, this pack. They're grays, though, or whites, like in the movies."

We watch until they disappear only feet from the ferry.

"They dived under the boat," Johnny says. We rush to the other side but they have disappeared.

"Stayed down," Johnny says. "Channel gets deeper as you go into the Strait. From here they'll go out the Strait past the reservation at the mouth, and on into the sea."

He stares reflectively after them. "I rode one once," he begins. "One of the big ones, ten feet and some. He was like a horse."

"I may be inexperienced, but I know when I'm being put on," I protest.

"No, you don't. It's true. It was a bet. I was twelve and pretty stupid. I needed a bike. The guys at the fishing dock said they'd chip in and buy me one if I'd do it. It wasn't as bad as it sounds. He was alone. Low tide had trapped him in a little bit of an inlet. He didn't have much room to maneuver and I think he was pretty old and weak. He had scars all over him and he was missing half a fin."

"Even then, he must have been hungry, waiting for the tide to come back. How could you do it? Weren't you scared?"

"First time in my life I was *white*. He still had all his teeth, or at least enough of them to do major damage to a dumb kid. I went out with the men to take a good look at him. His scales were as sharp as razor blades, and slippery besides. They'd have shredded my legs. I went home to get my older brother's catcher's padding. He wasn't home but my grandfather was. The old man got out of me what I was planning. He always could make me talk. He didn't say one word against it. He just thought a minute, very seriously, and told me to wait. He went out back to the shed where he kept a lot of weird stuff. He came back with a cottage cheese carton with a lid on it. Then he inspected my padding like he was going to be my second in a boxing match. He hummed and cleared his throat a lot, but finally nodded and off we went."

"You actually rode that shark?"

"I did. I was lucky getting on. That was tricky, but I landed on top of him first try. Took him by surprise. Even through the padding I could feel those scales like needles sticking into me. I had to hang on with bare hands, otherwise he was so slippery I could never have stayed on. I grabbed hold of that big old dorsal fin, or what was left of it, and froze to it. I've still got scars!" He shows me his hands. They are a road map of scars and calluses.

"He thrashed around trying to shake me. It was like riding a wild bull in a rodeo, only under water. I managed to stick on, but then I ran out of air. Only then did I figure that I had come to the hard part—getting off!"

"How did you do that?"

"My grandfather was watching from the boat, and when he figured it was time, he dumped the contents of that carton into the water ahead of the shark. I was lucky his aim was good. The shark's mouth hit that stuff before I did. He just about doubled up and went to the bottom. I let go and headed for the top as fast as I could go. The men pulled me up into the boat, and when I looked back I almost felt sorry for the poor sucker. He was heaving up everything he'd eaten for a week. He had no energy to waste on chasing a stupid, lucky kid."

"Did it kill him?"

"I don't think so. He disappeared at high tide. I think it just made him sick. But he was old anyway, and I'm sure it didn't do him any good. May have shortened his life some. I wasn't feeling particular. He could have shortened my life a whole lot."

"What was the stuff, do you know?"

"I have no idea. I only wish I'd had sense enough to ask what that stuff was. A good shark repellent would be worth a lot of money. I think one of the men asked, but he mumbled some word, I'm not even sure which dialect it was in, and he pretended not to know any English. I never bothered to learn my own language until two years ago. Grandfather was always going to teach me some of the stuff he knew, but you know how kids are. I had more important things to do. And then one evening my crazy cousin got drunk and challenged a loaded logging truck with his pickup. That was that. My grandfather and the dog were in the back of the pickup. They had to scrape them both off the pavement."

We are both quiet for awhile. It is a crazy story but I have no choice but to believe it. It is too wild to be anything but the truth. Finally, Johnny breaks the silence with a chuckle.

"My brother nearly killed me. His catcher's padding was ruined. Grandfather and I tried to clean it up but it was ripped, the stuffing was half gone, and the stains were permanent. I had to give him part interest in the bike or he'd have told my aunt. Grandfather never said a word about it. But those guys that put me up to it did. They're still telling it at Port Angeles. The story gets bigger every year and so does the shark!"

I stare at the water, trying to absorb the strangeness of the tale, and of a childhood I can not comprehend. What a difference the lack of common experience makes between this man and myself. At least Richard's background, though masculine, was familiar to me. I could relate to his difficulties, and to my children's. I look sideways in wonder and awe at the silent figure. How could I so instantly come to love this man, to hold him dearer than myself, and to abandon a lifetime of security to be with him and share his lifestyle? My god, he must be a legend! What other exploits, current ones, could he relate? What will he expect of me? I am only a mere mortal.

Ahead of us the Olympic Mountain range looms ever closer as we approach land. The majestic mountains stretch up into the clouds as if from the sea itself. Perhaps, growing up in their shadow, between the great forest and the vast Pacific Ocean, Johnny was shaped in a heroic mold. How will I ever live up to him?

SIX

We land at Kingston, a tiny resort town composed chiefly of ferry parking lot and marina. Johnny has picked up urgency in the landing process, as though his purpose is settled. His movements are controlled, his mind preoccupied. I hope it is sexual. I fear it is otherwise.

He heads west, toward the ocean, as fast as the motorcycle will comfortably go. I relax against his back, content to be carried along by his purposefulness, marveling at his capacity to go from dead rest to full speed with no apparent adjustment for inertia. I used to have a cat with that uncanny ability. He once caught a hummingbird in midflight.

Strangely, I am not even anxious to be enlightened about the reasons for Johnny's haste or his destination. I am happy to drift, to ride forever through the golden afternoon. It will be over soon enough. We will get to wherever we are speeding, and I am reasonably certain that I will be uncomfortable there. I no longer have the physical tolerance of the young, and I am without my vitamins!

Happiness takes some getting used to. This is the first time in my life that the present is all important to me. My life has been one long postponement, a continual expectation of better things that never happen. Now my past is over, and my future is a vague uneasiness like the purplish bruise of storm clouds behind the mountain range. Nothing exists but the two of us riding the cycle through the summer haze. The sun is warm on my back. We pass a cat dozing in the sun.

I smile at him, my brother in indolence. A little boy stares solemnly as we pass, yearning after the motorcycle.

I understand how he feels. It is a joy to ride on one. I had not known that before today. I never rode on a motorcycle. But I love it. I forbade my children the pleasure because motorcycles are dangerous. I suppress a silent twinge of guilt for depriving them. Oh well. Let them discover it for themselves. They rarely let my prohibitions interfere with their pleasures anyway. No other vehicle has ever given me the same thrill of movement, the shock of displaced wind on my face, the sensation of flying free, released from the limits of my own muscles. I am sure there are other ways to achieve the same experience—free falling from a plane, shooting the rapids, hang gliding—but I am not quite ready for those. . . . Or am I? Today, perhaps, I could do anything.

We accelerate to pass a pickup. The young driver grins enviously. I grin back, squeezing Johnny's waist. He is the most exiting birthday present I have ever had. So he is what I have been waiting for, ever since I was twenty-two dreaming of being forty-two and free of all my commitments. Old but free. I was convinced that I would be a dumpy, white-haired old woman. I had an image of myself, wrapped in a dark coat, riding in the back of buses, trains, planes, etc, all over the world, clutching my obligatory shopping bag. I look down at my jeans, my hiking boots, and to the motorcycle beneath me and chortle with relief and delight. I rub my cheek against my new lover's powerful back and allow myself the luxury of being touched by that twenty-two-year-old's quaintly warped vision of freedom. If only she could have had a glimpse of me this day. Would it have made her misery any easier to bear? Probably not. When I was a teenager my mother told me that I would be a late bloomer, that I would reach my peak late in life. It was little consolation. But then she was right. Discounting the scars of four births, I can pass for twenty-seven or twenty-eight. I am much better looking now than I was at sixteen. I look finished, complete. And, right now, I suspect I look radiant.

We pass a weathered gray sign offering "Live Vegetables." A bubble of laughter escapes my joy over this rural enthusiasm. The

Olympic Peninsula has always seemed insular, sheltered from progress by inaccessibility.

We have left behind the more developed resort communities near the ferry landing, and are deep into the older countryside. Here underbrush cleared years ago creeps back around frayed farms waiting sadly for the coming of bold new split-level hideaways. Between the farms stretch long undeveloped patches of new-growth pine and wildflowers: foxglove, daisies, Queen Anne's lace, and horsetail ferns. Sunny island meadows are grazed by an occasional cow. Behind these meadows rise the foothills, pine-draped or logged over, and beyond them, the mysterious, wild Olympic mountain range.

We pass an old gray farmhouse with a yard full of children. Their worn looking mother carrying an infant watches from the doorway as we pass. She grins and waves. I see no envy in her gesture, only acceptance. When I was in her shoes, my acceptance was more like resignation with a large helping of resentment. She is so young. There was an old nursery rhyme. . . . "There was an old woman who lived in a shoe. She had so many children. . . ." Perhaps this young woman is content, happy even. I once knew such a woman, Mrs. Wilcox. She had seven children. I went to sixth grade with one of her daughters, Evelyn. The Wilcoxes ran a mail-order candy business from their basement. The kids all worked there when they were old enough, along with their friends. The household drew stray children like flies, including me. It was a frantic, frayed existence. They lived in constant chaos and sticky disorder, but Mr. Wilcox did not seem to mind, and Mrs. Wilcox just sighed deeply, with contentment, and rearranged the mess.

I was always overwhelmed by their uproarious happiness and their normality. It made me feel like an outsider. I knew the Wilcox family for only a short time, and then we moved to the little house in the south Texas desert, and I thought often of them, with envy. But I have not thought of them in years. Even my own children did not call up that memory. I wonder why?

We pass a supermarket where carryout boys load grocery bags into battered station wagons. It is the *dinner hour*. I feel the familiar, almost atavistic urge to turn toward the nearest kitchen. Twenty years of training. Over. This is impossible to believe. A feeling of unreality replaces the guilt. Is this happening? It could not be. Any moment I will wake up back in my usual, constricted, uncomfortable reality. This is an incredible day, an earthquake day. It has shaken my life to its foundations and tossed my spirit free. On a day like this anything could happen. Electric forces charge the air. I have a sensation of movement more mysterious than that of the motorcycle's passage. Of movement through another medium; it makes me dizzy. I am going too fast. My mental computer cannot keep up with it.

Perhaps I am having heat prostration. My face burns uncomfortably. I have had too much sun and maybe even some windburn. My skin is sensitive. I do not tan; I gave up trying years ago. Normally, I hide behind glasses and hats. All this exposure is going to age me overnight. My recklessness has gotten me into an uncomfortable situation.

What is affecting me now is a different kind of exposure. And for it I will need more than hats and lotions. It will require the kind of protection I am deliberately abandoning, a blanketing security that filters a reality too harsh for delicate eyes. The shelter I was taught to seek as a small child.

Strange that I should have so readily accepted the role of greenhouse flower when inside I had always longed to be a participant. I always had little patience with people who sat on the sidelines and watched. I wanted to do things, to create, to make things happen. But I have *tried* to do that, even though from under a blanket, from inside a greenhouse. I *was* a participant. Johnny is right; I must give myself credit.

But I could have nurtured more of my talents instead of plunging into marriage and maternity with such a vengeance, overwhelming myself with it. What would my life have been like if I had chosen another path? I cannot imagine such an existence. I have only contempt for spinsterly isolation, for women who read about relationships instead of living them. I do not think I could have done that. I had to go all the way. To try it, to find out for myself. To reach for the happiness Mrs. Wilcox had.

This is a revelation to me. I have never thought of it like that. I really *chose* to have four children! I always felt I had no choice. I blamed it all on cultural expectations and on the lack of reliable birth control methods. But the choice was there. Maybe it was not a conscious choice. I certainly would not have chosen to have them all within four years like Mrs. Wilcox did. But I did choose. I could have *not* married, *not* had sex. I could have stayed in school and gotten a Ph.D. in psychology as I had planned. Or plunged myself into a career.

But I did not. I remember now, dimly without identification, as though it was something that happened to someone else. I wanted to experience *life* as I defined it then, to have close intimate relationships, sex, love, marriage, maternity. I envied Mrs. Wilcox desperately. Her mother had given her pride in her role as a woman. Mine bequeathed me bitterness and frantic ambition.

Eagerly, I left the outgrown parental roof to seek the sun. I sought it under another roof with even less freedom and overwhelming commitments. I spent twenty years filling other people's needs. Giving, giving, giving, and never satisfying my own needs. I am still hungering. Maybe this time.

We are passing through the outskirts of a town. There are restaurants and bars all around us, and the smell of charcoal-broiled steak reminds me sharply that I have not eaten since my Danish and coffee this morning. It is getting late and I am ravenous. I nudge Johnny. He half turns.

"Are we ever going to eat?" I yell.

He laughs shortly. "When there's time," he yells back and concentrates on the traffic.

Time from what? What sort of schedule are we on, I wonder? Well, I can stand to lose a few pounds. I have a feeling I will lose more than a few before this adventure is over. The crazy young man in front of me has other things on his mind than comfort. I hang on and concentrate on other things too, like the thought of his naked body. It is a comforting distraction. I am silently grateful for him, for this new chance at life. I know several women my age who are not so fortunate. With their children gone, they age daily, drying out as I watch, their feelings of usefulness over. Sucked dry by their off-spring, they rattle in the wind. I felt the chill of that same wind. For the moment that danger seems past. Maybe after this adventure I will be glad to sit in front of the TV and count the hours until it is time for my meds. But for the moment, I am going to live.

We are through the small town and turn off onto an old narrow road, sparsely traveled. Johnny's speed increases. I sense we are coming close to our destination and I shiver slightly. Within minutes we have left civilization altogether and are inside the deepest wilderness. The road, not much more than a logging road, seems to be the only sign of habitation. Trees meet overhead, and undergrowth threatens to take back the poorly maintained dirt road. We meet no more traffic.

We must be in the rain forest. It seems more like a green tunnel of time we are passing through. Club moss decorates every stump, and yellow-green ropes of selaginella drape the soaring trees. An eternal dripping silence wraps us, disturbed only by the roar of the motorcycle. I want to hush it, to tell Johnny to turn off the motor and to walk through the total silence.

The machine is necessary because Johnny feels a need for haste, and I must trust him. My life, for a time at least, depends on his wit and skill. I have not had such a strong feeling of dependency in years, of immediate trust in the whims and urgencies of another human being, of a man. I have become in the primal sense of the word, Johnny's woman. He is carrying me off with him to his cave. I revel in the ancient thrill of fear and pride.

Miles later we take another turning, an abrupt right this time onto a dirt road which is no more than a path. Giant ferns brush against us. Over the motor I hear another sound, one that seems as familiar as my heartbeat, the pounding of the sea against the rocks. I recognize it; I have been to the ocean before, in my former life, another world, with Richard and the children.

The path disappears altogether. Johnny stops the machine and gets off. We push the cycle up under the shelter of a rock outcropping and remove the saddlebags. Johnny covers the motorcycle carefully with a tarp, weighting it down with large rocks. He throws one of the saddlebags to me and hefts the other one. I stagger under the weight, which I judge to be about twenty-five pounds. I used to be pretty good at figuring the weight of babies and grocery bags.

"That's the light one," he replies to the expression on my face. "Storm tonight. The tide's still in too high to ride any further. My timing gets thrown off when I go back to town. We won't make it all the way in; we'll have to camp out."

"In a storm? Are you sure? Did you hear a weather report or something?" The sky, what I have seen of it, has been clear and the afternoon sunny. The clouds over the mountains came and went, traveling eastward.

Johnny snorts with deep contempt, "Weather report! Storm's coming. Move it, woman, if you want to eat tonight."

His instruction is compelling. I shift my burden and follow him down a narrow trail through the brush, sloshing through a swampy runoff and down a sharp incline toward the beach. I hesitate a moment to take a deep breath of the sharp salt air gusting up the little draw, and then hurry to catch up. His urgency has become mine.

SEVEN

The first time I saw the Pacific Ocean I cried. The real thing, the
pure sweep of wind and waves all the way from the orient completely undid me. The wind is a physical assault. The wild roar of
waves exploding against the beach is overwhelming. Down the coast
in California, the uniform blue water and white sand look theatrical.
But off the wild Olympic Peninsula, the ocean looks and feels like the
impressive weight of water that it is, dark and cold, beautiful but
potentially deadly.

On this trip, with Johnny, I am moved even more deeply because
I am out of context, unnaturally stimulated. But I have little leisure
to enjoy the experience. Johnny takes off across the logs and I scramble after him, trying to catch my breath in the intoxicating air. He is
moving swiftly, his feet sure on the logs. But then, he played as a child
on these beaches. This is his home territory. Mine was the cornfields
of Iowa and the bone-dry flatlands of South Texas. I slip and wobble
and turn my ankle jumping awkwardly from one log to the next. He
stops finally and waits for me to catch up.

"Stay with me," he says. "When I go into the woods, you have to
follow me closely. If you get lost, you could stay lost. I might never
find you."

"Then slow down," I yell to his retreating back. He does not
pause, but I know he hears me. I try to keep up, meditating on his
message, scarcely able to believe it. He is not joking. I have learned
that much about this man. I have to take his words literally. He is in

a hurry, and I must be also. My life probably depends on it. At least I must act as though it did. His pace does not slow for me, and he will not repeat his warning. He trusts me to have sense enough to do as I am told. I can do it. I have been a wife, following a man, stifling my questions, postponing my objections, and hustling. It is difficult enough to keep up; all my attention is taken by my footing, but I do not dare lose sight of Johnny.

Suddenly, he is gone. I search desperately for a landmark, fixing my eyes on a fallen tree as I scramble to reach the place where he has vanished. There is no discernable path through the brush, away from the beach. I take a deep breath and plunge into the permanent chill of the deep rain forest.

I fight hard to recover him. Johnny is not kidding about getting lost. The trees and undergrowth grow so thickly that I could disappear completely in minutes. I remember stories I have read in the newspapers about people who disappeared on the Peninsula and were never found. Planes crash regularly and the remains vanish forever. The thicket of berries and ferns and the carpet of rotted pine needles muffle sound. I can hear nothing but the eternal dripping silence. I have never heard such silence. An occasional bird cries unfamiliarly overhead. Moisture drops continually from the roof of branches. It trickles underfoot in intermittent streams. I can no longer hear the ocean though we cannot be far from it. I am relieved to hear Johnny just a few feet ahead breaking a path through the undergrowth. He moves surely, but I feel lost.

Eerie green moss drips from every branch. Club moss coats everything else, turning the forest into a hairy living thing. A rustle in the ferns nearby startles me. Johnny laughs. He has sensed my fear from some distance ahead.

"Ground squirrel," he yells back. "Tastes a little like rat!"

I make a face at his back. I am shivering in spite of my heavy jacket. Hunger is eating up my internal organs. The pace is straining my undisciplined muscles, and my hands and face are bleeding from scratches where the devil's club has brushed against me. I wonder what Johnny is looking for. The woods all look the same to me—forbidding.

Then he stops. "Here," he says, pointing through the trees.

"Terrific," I say, as I wonder what is so special about this spot. "Now what?" I ask.

He grunts. I have noticed that his speech has been deteriorating since we hit the wilds, becoming monosyllabic. It is undoubtedly the urgency of the moment. I hope so.

Johnny begins clearing a space of undergrowth with the implement he has been using on the path and I see for the first time that it is a rough stone axe, reasonably sharp, bound with leather straps to a wooden handle that was not made by machine. He must have taken it out of his saddlebag. He does not offer me one, so I find a sharp rock and a pointed stick and try to help. I run into another patch of devil's club and slash myself on its vicious thorns, trying not to cry. I am beginning to feel sorry for myself again. Johnny works steadily, ignoring me. My puny efforts make little impact on the enormous job. Incredibly, he is slicing through the brush, methodically clearing it away. I give up trying to do what he does and follow behind him, piling up what he cuts away. He does not comment on my activities, but I feel approval. I am picking up vibrations more quickly in this stillness.

As we work, I notice that behind all the blueberry and salal and ferns is a large outcropping of rock, almost a fortress.

"Where's the beach?" I ask with sudden clearing of vision.

Johnny points beyond the rock. This time he does not even make a sound. I grunt my understanding, meaning it to sound mocking, but it merely sounds appropriate. Besides, I am tired and talking takes energy.

We have been traveling parallel to the beach, apparently, and the rock formation will form a windbreak for our camp, protecting it from the storm coming off the ocean. When, miraculously, a space has been cleared inside a semicircle of giant trees around the land side of the rock, Johnny draws a wide circle in the dirt and, taking the sharp rock and the pointed stick I was using, demonstrates how to break up the clods of forest floor with them. He finds a spade-shaped piece of bark to use as a scoop to clear out the dirt from a shallow ditch, throwing it inside the circle.

"Drainage ditch," he volunteers with an extravagant use of words. "Build it higher on the inside. I'll be back." He hands me the rude tools and sets off with his axe.

My back already aches from bending over, clearing brush, but I set about the task appointed me. The fact that he has vanished and I cannot hear him makes me uneasy. I have no choice but to cling to his promise to return. I feel totally lost. I work hard to quell my nervousness, determined to finish the job he has set me before he returns.

The ground is mostly humus, hundreds, maybe thousands of years worth of vegetation with yellow clay underneath. The primitive tools are slow, but I discover that having a rhythm helps make some progress. I work from the outside, squatting and rising at intervals to trample clods inside the circle to ease my back. Johnny comes back, dumps a load of poles he has somehow cut, or perhaps trimmed from a fallen tree, looks at my work, grunts approval, and disappears again. I feel unreasonably pleased as well as relieved by his momentary presence.

Johnny returns several times carrying poles, brush, and an enormous chunk of well-aged tree trunk. By the time he has finished I am nearly done with my work. I am ridiculously proud of the tiny ditch. It wavers slightly from the circle and is smaller than I intended, but I have done it myself. I finish it while he plants poles just inside the circle. One of the poles is forked to support the opposite ones. Some still have branches attached, which also support the others. He reinforces the skeleton with lashings of vine. He borrows my rock to pound one pole in and suggests that I make runoffs from my ditch toward the water. I am angry with myself for not having considered such a simple thing. Of course there have to be runoffs, otherwise the ditch would fill up with water and flow over and we would be no better off than if we had no ditch at all. Johnny makes no editorial comment, but I am ashamed. I dig furiously.

Occasionally, as Johnny works, he looks toward the place where the sky would be if the trees were not in the way. He is weaving hemlock and balsam branches through the framework. Turning them over, I can see that they form a reasonably waterproof shield that way.

Finally, he comments. "It's getting late. Bring some of that clay you just dug up and help me plaster the bottom, especially in the back. That rock is going to drip some. We've still got to get more firewood."

Plastering I am better at. I find a tiny stream nearby and fill a large maple leaf with water to soften up the clay. There is mint growing along the stream. I take a drink hesitantly and then enthusiastically. The water is cold and minty. It makes up for a lot of missing conveniences. It seems a shame to waste it on mud. It could be bottled and sold. . . . Forget it. I hurry back. Johnny is almost finished.

I am allowed to go with him to help carry firewood. He is cutting up a fallen alder, using my rock as an edge to split the rotting chunks of fat wood for the fire. Around us are several downed trees, some not so old. One giant hemlock near us has fallen so recently that the root wheel still drops clods of dirt.

"Why did it fall?" I ask.

"Shallow roots. Tree got too tall. Wind blew it over. A bad storm blows down lots."

I sight along the length of the trunk and imagine the giant crashing through the trees. "Wow!" I comment with awe.

Johnny grins as he picks up one pile of wood.

"What if ? . . ." I begin.

He anticipates my question. "That's one reason I picked our campsite," he answers. "A tree would have to fall horizontally across the shelter to bring it down. The rocks protect us every other direction, and there's enough rock projection on the flanks to keep the direct force of a fall off us. Hurry up. We've got to move."

I am impressed. I move. Our shelter looks almost professional. I congratulate him.

"It's not much," Johnny says modestly. "It's temporary. An emergency shelter. My ancestors would have done much better. If you were traveling with a woman, you'd probably have cedar mats with you. Unless, of course, you'd just stolen her unexpectedly."

His deadpan makes me laugh. But he continues seriously.

51

"There's not much here to work with. Further south we'd have cedar bark. That makes good shingles. I could have made a shed in an hour with that."

Johnny finishes stacking the wood around the inside walls for extra protection. He dumps the large old log in a shallow hole he scoops in the center of the house and surrounds it with rocks for a fireplace. We have a piece of loose brush for a door, and we pile balsam boughs opposite the door and cover them with dry moss and the huge green leaves of a big-leaf maple. It makes a tolerable bed.

I can see that the light outside is weakening. Building the shelter has taken a long time.

"Dinner," Johnny announces and leads me down an invisible path to the beach. I am surprised to see how close we are to the water, only about five minutes away. The waves seem higher now than they had been, but they are much further out.

"Tide's out far enough. Table is spread," Johnny says.

I look anxiously at the cold, wet scene, and at the clouds piling up visibly now on the horizon. It hardly looks appetizing. From an inner pocket, Johnny produces a fine-meshed bag like a gunny sack, pulls off his boots, socks, jeans, and jacket, and stashes them behind a rock near the path. I follow his example, without question.

Although it is getting late, the light is still strong enough to see. This far west it lingers in the summer. We wade out until the water is just over our knees. Johnny bends over and begins to feel around in the surf, softly crooning some language I do not understand. In a minute he makes a quick scooping gesture and brings up a razor clam. He drops it into the bag that he has tied around his waist.

I exclaim appropriately. I tried razor claming once before and I appreciate the miracle I have just witnessed! Razor clams move with lightning speed and are impossible for a layman to catch. Johnny repeats the performance three times before I start to feel useless standing up to my knees in freezing water and decide to try. Nothing. I come up with several stones, old empty shells, seaweed, driftwood, and a lot of empty sand.

I look at Johnny. "What are you saying?" I demand.

"I'm talking to them in their language," he says, putting another clam in his bag.

"But what are you saying to them?" I insist.

He looks me straight in the face and repeats, in English, "'Come little brothers, jump into my hands or your mother-in-law will get you,' roughly translated, of course. It's the clam-hunting song my tribe uses."

I laugh until I fall over with the force of a wave. Johnny shrugs and goes back to his crooning and raking in the elusive clam harvest. I stop laughing. However foolish it may sound, it works. So I try it myself, in English. Either my language is too harsh, or I do not sound sincere. I still come up empty handed.

"I don't speak clam," I confess to Johnny. "They don't care much for English."

"The language doesn't matter. You have to feel like a clam, be a clam," Johnny offers, seriously. "You find them by feel, sort of coax them into your hands."

I try. Being a clam is not easy. They live in an alien environment. I do not enjoy being a clam, but after awhile I feel a motion by my foot, a sifting of sand not explainable by the surf. I reach there and touch something flat and sharp and pull up my first razor clam. I look at it in amazement.

"I did it!" I yell. I put my offering into Johnny's half-full bag with disproportionate pride. Johnny grins.

"You're going to make a first-class squaw," he says. "You've got clam mentality."

I am into the hunt. It is exhilarating, chasing the slippery mollusks, a real challenge, and the object is to feed my starving stomach. I forget the cold, the sharpness of the rocks, and the pain in my hands and arms and face from salt water in the devil's club scratches. I forget who I was and who I am. I become part of the eerie twilight, one with the golden brown oval clam shell. I sink down into a part of myself I did not know existed. I become part of the hunt.

I am clucking to the clams as though they are chickens, soothing, calling to them, making feeding noises, moving my waiting open hands, moving them ever so gently, rhythmically in a raking motion, and I am catching clams. I learn to distinguish the feel of a clam from a rock almost immediately. Soon I can sense a clam's presence. My mind is disengaged. I have become an atavistic predator. After centuries of disuse, the hunting instinct is still present in me.

I keep careful count of my catch, nine razor and a geoduck, that prehistoric obscenity of a giant clam. It is Johnny's turn to howl with laughter at the sight of my face when I come up with the geoduck.

"You're a natural," Johnny says with some astonishment.

"I'm not as fast as you are."

"Takes practice. You should watch my aunt. She's been doing it since she was a child. She could fill this sack in a quarter of the time it takes both of us to do it. Clamming is women's work, anyway. Traditionally, of course," he adds hastily. "Remind me. Tonight I'll tell you the story of the Clam Woman."

I catch my crab almost accidentally. I am so focused on looking for clams that I almost let it get away, but the food gathering instinct saves me. I pull up the fat, reddish brown body in wonder and I hold on despite the waving claws. Dungeness crabs seem to be traveling together. In another minute Johnny picks up two more. He shows me the difference between male and female, throwing the female one back. The bottom shell on the female is broader than the male's. Naturally.

Our sack is nearly full. The tide has retreated even further and we have followed it until we reach a formation of rocks inhabited by gulls, a long way from shore. Johnny wades over to the rocks. The light is almost gone. He pulls out his knife, a wicked looking thing with a long, stone blade and proceeds to pry oysters off the rocks. I watch closely, trying to distinguish between the mussels, the barnacles, and the oysters, all of which are encrusted with the same patchy white, lime coating. I have to give up. The light is not good enough. I am confident that another day when the light is better I will manage that knack also. I feel invincible. I have caught nine of the "uncatchable" razor clams. I can feed myself in the wild if I have to. And just now, it seems that I must.

The weather has changed abruptly. Suddenly it is dark. The sky is black with storm, and the ocean is pounding us. A wave splashes up to our chins and Johnny gives up and motions toward the shore with his head. As we wade back, he grabs some floating seaweed, a long piece of it, and hands it to me to carry. He is shouldering the now heavy sack of seafood. I can almost float back on my elation. I grab yet another length of kelp and bundle it carefully with the first. I imagine it is for wrapping the shellfish to cook.

The wind is blowing harder and the waves mount, exploding on the rocks. I look back. The sea is deep over the place we have just left. I understand why the oysters are cemented to their rocks. Powerful surges test their moorings. I move as fast as I can go, suddenly cold with fear. We are a long way from shore, and it has become a race. Johnny is struggling a little, weighted by his burden. Lightning dances on the waves around us. Thunder bursts over the noise of the waves. We are finally out of the pounding surf and race across the flat, wet sand toward shelter. Rags of foam, like soap scum, chase us across the sand.

The first drops of rain feel warm after the salt spray. We crawl behind the rocks to pull on our clothing, not stopping to lace boots in our haste. The rain is soaking as we head for the shelter of the woods, gales of hell at our heels. Once inside the trees the rain is lighter, but the wind howls louder through the tops of the trees. We race, laughing, to our little shelter, and crawl inside gratefully. Johnny sets down his bag of dinner with a deep sigh of relief. All those wet shells are heavy!

We are shivering with excitement and cold. We pull the makeshift door to, shutting out the storm. Inside it is dark and cold and drafty. We hug each other in the dimness and laugh gently.

"I hope you've got a match," I plead. "We'll die of pneumonia before you get a spark out of two sticks!"

"Hell, woman, I'm the fastest fire maker in the west. Just watch my smoke!" He takes a rawhide bootlace, and a pair of dry sticks and some moss, and in minutes has coaxed a spark onto the moss. In seconds a flame catches the rotted log. It smokes badly. In spite of the dozens of escape holes in the rude shelter, smoke fills the little space. I cough, but Johnny does not seem to notice. He sets about tending the fire and bundling our dinner up in the long strands of wet kelp. The space inside the hut warms quickly in spite of the gusting of the wind through the cracks. I learn to appreciate the gust, which thins out the smoke. I take off my damp clothes and try to dry them and warm my icy body by the fire.

The rotting, punky wood in the old log burns quickly, while the smaller stuff takes longer to catch. It is a long time before Johnny is satisfied with the fire. He wants nothing less than a pile of glowing coals to cook with. Johnny splits the crabs, wraps them like the clams, and we heap the bundles on the hot coals carefully so as to not smother the fire. Johnny starts a small fire on top of the bundles.

While we wait for the clams and crab to cook, Johnny opens the oysters, and we gulp them raw. I find to my amazement that they slip down easily if they are fresh and you are hungry. When the fire has died down, Johnny brushes the coals away and we gingerly poke out the bundles and eat the hot shellfish. The shells have all opened, and the clams are sandy but delicious. Everything has its own briny flavor from the salt water and the kelp and is so fresh it does not need any other seasoning. It tastes like it has been soaked in butter. I am ravenous. I consider cheerfully that by eating nothing but seafood once a day and working this hard to get it, I will be lean and starved looking before the week is out. I stuff my face, lick my fingers, and laugh like a child at the sight of the two of us gorging ourselves.

Johnny builds up the fire when we have finished eating, and shoves the remains of our feast, shells mostly, out the door into the rain.

"I'll take the shells back to the beach in the morning," Johnny explains. I listen to the crashing of the wind in the trees around us and am glad he does not feel compelled to go now.

We have eaten everything edible, including most of the monstrous geoduck, which is tough and has a faint flavor of turpentine. We lie back on our improvised bed and listen to the storm roar outside.

Johnny begins the promised story.

One day a woman was walking along the beach crying, when she tripped over the largest clam she had ever seen. She started to cry even harder because she had hurt her foot on the clam's sharp shell.

"'Why are you crying, you clumsy woman?' the clam asked, crossly.

"Because I have no man, no one to take care of me. I will starve. My man was drowned by a sea lion and my family is tired of looking after me."

"'I am looking for a wife,' the clam said. 'If you will be my wife, you may come live with me and I will take care of you.'

So the woman went to live with the giant clam under the sea. He lived in a large village of clam people, where he was the head man because of his size. He was good to the woman, and she had many children by him, but she was not happy. She was wet and cold all the time and missed the comforts of her other, human world. As she got older she got more and more quarrelsome, and more difficult to get along with. Finally, she had a big fight with her daughter and her daughter's husband. Her son-in-law, who was now the ruler of the clam people, became so angry that he took the woman back to the beach where the giant clam had found her and left her there. The woman was furious because she had been badly treated by her son-in-law. In revenge she went back to her own village and taught the women the secrets of the clam people. Our women have been able to catch clams easily ever since.

I break into the silence. "The moral of that story is, if I get hard to live with, you will throw me back. But beware, I might tell my people all your secrets." I am too sleepy to be anything but amused by the story.

"The moral is, don't take a woman from another world."

"Then you aren't paying attention to your own myth."

"I know. But I felt sorry for you. You looked so lost."

"You could have given me directions. You didn't feel that sorry for me. Why did you bring me?"

"Why did you come?" he retorts. "Don't ask questions. It's happening; that's all that's important. Relax and enjoy my lovemaking; or did you come all this way just to catch clams?"

I have so many questions. Unasked. Unaskable? I am too tired, and Johnny's arms are too comfortable. I allow myself to submerge into the warmth and closeness of him and our mutual need. We are alone in our little cave of firelight in the blackness of the world. There is nothing outside demanding our attention, no responsibilities, no concerns except the storm, which just makes it cozier inside. There are no background noises of TV, radio, cars, people; only the howling of the wind and beyond it the thunder and the pounding of the surf. Inside there is only Johnny's warmth and his urgency.

Again Johnny seems to read my desires, anticipating my needs. His hands are gentle, tender, and insistent. I am not allowed to stray from our purpose. I am tended like the fire, harvested like the clams. Surrender to delight is easy and inevitable. I understand why he caught three clams to my one. If I were a clam, I too, would throw myself into his hands. He begins the chant. I feel even more like his catch, lured by his song into his net. And I go gladly, eagerly, joyously in spite of aching muscles, frozen bones, unbalanced diet, and total disorientation, or culture shock. I throw myself as wantonly into the passion of lovemaking as I had into the clam hunt earlier. I become a part of this strange and wonderful creature beside me, all male, all pleasure, whose mind and motives are as totally foreign to me as if he had dropped out of a time warp, from another era. I enter into the essence of him, and understand maleness. I feel both male and female at once, his pleasure intermingling with mine.

And then it all drops away. I cling to him, gorged and dripping, and sleep.

EIGHT

Where am I? My God, what have I done? An arctic cold has wakened me. My blood feels like frozen slush in my veins. The fire is out. Johnny? Am I alone? I hear him outside. I have been sleeping on a hard, wet pile of brush that jabs me in several places. The drafty playhut is wet inside and smells strongly of smoke and decaying clams. And above everything else, the cold is numbing me from the inside out.

How did I get myself into this mess? I stir and remember last night. Well. That answers that question. But I am not the type of woman to go chasing after a young man's body. Or am I? I am here. No fool like an old fool?. . .

How could I do such a thing? What would my friends think? My family? Richard? . . . God. If I go back immediately, no one would ever have to know.

But I do not want to go back. I seem to have slammed that door shut, firmly and finally. Maybe camping out in the woods is not what I want. But whatever it is, it will be what *I* want and not what other people want for me. From now on my life will be a present to me from me. No more wrong sizes, wrong styles, useless trivia, or someone else's noise and confusion filling my quiet. It will be my life, tailor made, right or wrong. And I am turning out to have a lot more imagination than I ever dreamed.

I giggle and get up quickly. How many times have I giggled in the last twenty four hours? I have to get warm. My clothes are damp and *literally* clammy. I am shivering and hurry out into the newly washed day.

"Shouldn't we build up the fire?" I ask.

"Why? We're leaving."

"I'm freezing."

"Move around. You'll warm up."

"Breakfast? Something hot?"

Johnny looks at me with patient amusement. "You want a piece of geoduck? I think there was a little left," he says.

I make a face. "No! I want coffee and toast and eggs and bacon and . . ."

Johnny shrugs and points. "Civilization is that way," he says.

I sigh deeply and retire into the bushes to relieve myself. This relationship is not going to be easy. How could I ever have gotten involved with a man who does not need coffee in the morning? I knew my new life was going to be somewhat uncomfortable, but no more hot coffee, regular meals, hot showers? . . .

I cross the campsite to the stream and have a deep drink of the minty fresh water. I splash my face and hands with it. That helps. I stretch. I feel lean and fit and hungry. Damned savage. I grin with satisfaction. The trouble is, I feel good. I feel great. For someone who could never sleep in anything but my own bed, I have slept better than I can remember. That is the sex. I comb my tangled hair and weave it into two braids, shrugging aside the symbolism. It is the simple thing to do. Besides, I do it at home sometimes when I am working outside. I look at my face in the compact mirror. I look awful. . . . Well, different. Younger? Maybe a little. That is the sex, too. I consider makeup. For whom? Not for a man who will not give me a cup of coffee. He wants things primitive, he'll get primitive. Including an older woman who would look more appealing in makeup. Tough. He will take me the way I am or take me back. I wish I had some face cream, though. I am beginning to feel dried out.

Hunger is a great inspiration. I trip over some blueberry bushes while thrashing around in the mint. Delighted, I gather as many as I can before Johnny comes looking for me.

He laughs when he sees what I am doing. "You're going to sur-vive," he says. "You're going to do just fine. For a non-Indian, you're a natural savage!"

Funny he should use that term. I just applied it to him. Is he reading my mind? Again? I look at him sideways, my mouth full of berries. I will not need lipstick today.

He reaches out to touch my cheek, very gently. I am so moved I stop eating.

"I'm glad I brought you," he says. "Now come on. Time to go. The tide won't wait on your stomach."

What can I do? I follow him. I would follow him anywhere, I *am* following him anywhere. This is as close to the ends of the earth as I will probably ever get.

Johnny picks up the heavier saddlebag and tosses me the other one. He sets off away from camp. I pick up my burden and follow. I have little choice. I could never find my own way back. And I am pretty sure I do not want to. But boy do I want a cup of coffee!

Freedom! Bah! I had hoped I was finally free of the physical sex trap. My body is full of surprises. Here we go again, following yet another man, this time a younger one, a more demanding one, at his whim and disposal. Following the indecipherable map he has in his head. I do as I am told. The only choice I have made so far is to fol-low him. To trust him. And that was a biggie. But I am not sorry. He is blunt and brusque but infinitely tender, and I do not begin to understand him. Maybe if I am patient. . . .

It is colder than last night. The forest drips and squishes with new vigor and the wind is fresh. There are several newly fallen trees in our path and lots of branches torn from others. We pass more berry bushes, salmonberries, blackberries and more blueberries. They might as well not be there. Johnny will not let up his pace and I do not dare fall behind to pick them. He will not look back to check on me. It is up to me to keep going. It is hard; I am rested, but so is he.

We walk a long time. My load is heavy. I am definitely going to have to toughen up if I am going to live like this. I hope that wher-ever we are going has *some* of the amenities of civilization. Like a coffee pot. It is terrible to be so dependent on little things. Comfort did not mean all that much to me when I was very young. I learned to hate camping out because of the children. But that was my old life. My new life seems to involve a whole new set of values. And comfort is not on the list. Sex is way up there though, and self reliance, skill, competence with my hands, endurance, and probably courage.

I look around me. While I have been musing my subconscious has been at work, trying to warn me, and the warning has suddenly become conscious. I am really learning how to listen. The stillness has spoken to me. It is always quiet, but now it is eerily so. Not even a bird cries. Johnny's pace has slowed. I open my mouth to comment, and he puts his hand up before I can speak. This telepathic stuff is beginning to get to me. He stops altogether and signals me to stop where I am. He does not need to. He is pulling out his knife and I am dead still, waiting. Slowly, carefully, he moves ahead until he is out of sight.

I stay put as instructed, my heart making a racket in my ears. This is such alien country I am not even sure what the possibilities might be. Wild animals, surely. Unfriendly humans, possibly. Anything more is beyond my imagining. I am not superstitious, but the world I move in now is beyond my experience. And I am beginning to operate in it in a way I would not have thought possible.

Where is Johnny? It is taking him a long time. If something should happen to him, what would become of me? I am working up a good case of nerves when he appears quite close and signals me to follow, quietly. We strike out at an angle to our original direction, Johnny moving slowly and soundlessly. I try to imitate him but it is much harder than it appears. The salal thicket rustles whenever I brush against it, and since it is everywhere, it is impossible not to touch it. A branch crackles under my feet, and I continually trip over tree roots. If it were not for the soundproof carpet of rotting vegetation it would be hopeless.

Finally, we seem to be cutting back in the other direction, and after awhile Johnny's pace is back to normal and we are making headway. I am trying to listen to the forest, to determine if we are well past the danger, and I find we are back at the motorcycle we left the

night before. This confuses me totally. I was certain we were traveling in the other direction.

"What was that back there?" I demand.

"Bear. Mother and half-grown cub. In the blueberries. A black
bear, probably not a threat, but no point in disturbing them."

Johnny loads the bags back on the cycle. There is something
wrong about that. Something that has been disturbing me all morning. It comes to me all at once. It is the bags.

"What's in those bags?" I ask, "that is so important that we had
to carry them all that way and bring them back again? I only saw you
take out an axe and a knife, which you could have carried."

He grins sheepishly. "Blankets, tarp, clothes."

"But we could have used those blankets last night! And a tarp
would have helped with the shelter! Johnny?!!"

"Didn't want to spoil you. Didn't you enjoy last night?"

"Sure, but . . . !"

"I wanted to show you what it was like. All of it. The 'old way.'
Just you and me and our own hands."

"Then why bring the gear along at all?"

"Just in case we had problems. Besides, carrying a load will help
toughen you up."

"Goddamn you. Don't you do that to me again. Don't you trust
me at all?"

"I'm beginning to." He wheels the machine down to the beach.
I follow him, carrying my anger.

When we reach the sand and clear the pile of logs, he gets on
and motions for me to get on behind him. I do so. I am at least grateful to be riding.

"Tide's out again. We ride," he says, and starts the cycle. We take
off over the wet sand. Johnny heads straight for the water, hits some
standing water and slides sideways to the edge of the waves. I catch
my breath, but he is laughing. I can feel the muscles in his belly
harden. It excites me. Damn him. I lay my cheek on his back and feel
my throat sob with a sudden tremor. God, how I love this man! And,
as usual, he knows. He reaches back to pinch me.

"Keep your hands on the handlebars!" I fuss, but he is forgiven and he knows it.

We make good time. It is freezing with the freshened air streaming past, but it is exhilarating and the sun makes it tolerable. The air is like champagne, burning and tickling at the same time. It makes us laugh. We ride on and on and I can not help being grateful that I do not have to walk the distance. We race down the beach, dodging flotsam left by the storm. We splash through tiny inlets where the runoff from the forest trickles into the sea. We chase the gulls, laughing and yelling at their protests with the pure pleasure of motion.

Then the ride is over. We come around a point into a lovely inlet and are in Johnny's permanent camp. There is no mistaking it. I am not sure what I was expecting, but it wasn't this. Culture shock, which has been massing on the horizon for the last twenty-four hours, hits me with the fury of last night's storm. I get off the bike, walk over to a driftwood log, sit down, and cry. Johnny stands looking at me, not knowing whether to be hurt, disgusted, or amused. I am aware that I must pull myself together to make things all right with him. But I cannot, just yet.

This is going to be my home, for awhile, at least, if I am going to stay with Johnny. And I want to do that. It is truly like going back two thousand years. I know that is what Johnny has intended. I am sure he worked very hard to achieve that effect. He was devastatingly successful. It is an Indian camp. The earliest Spanish explorers might have seen just such a sight as they rounded the tiny inlet in their sailing ships.

Parallel to the beach Johnny has built a long, low, wooden shed-like building of what looks like long planks in a curious overlapping shingle construction. The whole structure looks as fragile as though a giant child had constructed it of wooden cards, and at the same time it seems as immutable as time. It has weathered to a soft silver and is supported by massive carved pole supports covered with fierce images. Drying racks fill the beach around the house, and fishing gear is piled everywhere: lines, nets, poles, and a long spear that could be a harpoon. Past the tide line on the beach, upside down, are two boats, one larger than the other and carved and painted and breath-takingly beautiful. All this scene needs are kids and dogs and squaws gathering firewood.

The total effect is imposing and terrifying. It is like a museum scene brought to life. Johnny finally kneels beside me and puts his arms around me.

"Hey, it's all right," he says. "If you want to go back, I'll take you. Don't cry for crissakes. I should never have brought you!"

I cling to him. I cannot quit crying, but in between sobs I manage to blurt out what is uppermost in my mind. "I know now how they felt," I blubber. "All those women."

"What women?"

"The wives I read about. When the white settler's wives first came to this area, they all stepped ashore and looked around and sat down and cried!"

Johnny decides to laugh, and then I am laughing with him at the same time I am crying. It is a sloppy mess, but it relieves the tension. After awhile Johnny goes away to build a fire inside the house. He brings me some hot water in a watertight basket. I taste it and make a face.

"What is it?"

"Pine needle tea. Lots of vitamin C."

Somehow scurvy is the last of my concerns. He brings out some pilot crackers and a chunk of smoked salmon. I wolf that down and drink some more tea and stop crying.

"I'm sorry, Johnny. That was unforgivable. I couldn't help it, though. It was too much all at once. It's an incredible camp. You know that. It isn't that I don't like it, or that I don't appreciate what you've done here. I do. And I'm going to be very happy here. I know it. You've just got to give me time to get used to it all. It's a helluva long jump from Queen Anne Hill!"

Johnny looks around and grins. "I'm used to it," he admits. "But it does seem to have strange effects on other people."

"Do you bring many people here?"

"Almost nobody." His tone puts an end to that subject.

"How can you afford to leave things outside like that?" I ask, changing the subject. For now. "Doesn't anybody steal around here?"

Johnny points out to the mouth of the inlet where the sea foams around hidden rocks. I had not noticed them as we came in.

"This is reservation land," he explains. "It is so remote that it is pretty well protected by land, and the rocks keep me safe from curious boaters. I'm the only one in the world who knows how to get in here safely by water."

"Aren't there any marine charts?"

"Not on this part of the res."

"Can I go inside now?" I ask, almost shyly.

Johnny nods and conducts the tour. The longhouse is not much more than the drafty rectangular shed it looks from outside. It has a dirt floor, and surprisingly few cracks. It is dark and smoke-stained and the little fire Johnny has built does little to brighten the gloom. I can make out sleeping and sitting benches along the sides. The rafters are for storage. Strange things hang there, moving slowly, softly like cobwebs in the draft. I shudder and gulp. There are too many impressions and I am afraid I am going to cry again.

Johnny leads me back out into the sunlight. We sit on the driftwood and Johnny puts his arm around me and holds me.

"I have tried to make everything myself, the way my ancestors did it. It's not easy any more. So many of the skills took years to develop and were highly specialized; only one person in the tribe would perfect each skill. The techniques died with the craftsmen."

"That's exciting and historically commendable, I'm sure. But why go to all this trouble? What's in it for you?"

His tone is slightly defensive. "I'm looking for the image of myself in the dust of my ancestors, I suppose. Sometimes I feel close, but when I reach out, it is only a shadow."

"Where do I fit in?"

"It's a bachelor's camp. It needs a woman. There are things I can't do. Things that you will know instinctively how to do."

His vision is becoming clear to me. I know why he has brought me here, why he needs me—to complete the picture he has so painstakingly painted.

"But why me?" I can't quite strain the plaintiveness out of my tone. "Wouldn't a woman from your own tribe be better?"

His eyes shutter tight. His voice is hard. "No!" he says, ending that enquiry. So he has tried that and it did not work. With a vengeance, I would guess. That explains a lot of things, but still fails to explain me. Except that I was willing to come. I needed this man and he needed me. There is more, a lot more that I still do not understand.

I am on very dangerous ground with him now. One misstep and I could lose him. I feel my way carefully. "That's asking a lot of me, Johnny. I'm not sure I can live up to it. I don't want to disappoint you."

He shrugs. "I know that I am asking the impossible. But you are the impossible. I will appreciate any effort you make. I don't think you are going to disappoint me. I think you are going to amaze yourself. I think you already have."

I nod, not trusting my voice.

"It is the custom in my world," he begins softly, "for a young man to go into the forest alone to seek his spirit and to ask for a vision that will show him how the pattern of his life is woven into the larger pattern of his world."

He gets up and paces tensely. "I find this difficult to translate for your ears," he explains. "In my vision I was standing on the ocean's shore, waiting and watching. One day after a storm, a cedar log washed up on the sand in front of me. It turned into a beautiful woman. I mated with the woman, and as we lay in each other's arms the earth turned white with a blinding light. We turned our eyes away in fear but we were safe as long as we were together.

"When I got back home I told my vision to my grandfather, who believed in such things. He was very pleased.

"I asked my grandfather what it all meant. I'm trying to remember exactly what he said. Something about the dreams being very important, not only to us but to the whole tribe and maybe other tribes as well. We could not understand it all then, he said, but when the time was right it would become clear.

"I have tried to be patient. But I searched for two years along the shore for the exact place I saw in my vision, where I waited for the log woman. This is it. You're sitting on it. I built my house here and settled down to wait."

"You're waiting for a cedar log to wash up on your shore and turn into a woman?"

Johnny chuckles. "That's not nearly as funny as the next part. When I first saw you I knew you were the woman in my vision."

"I looked like a cedar log?"

"Of course not. But in a way, yes. You looked different, special. Your hair is long and the color of cedar. No. You look like the woman the log became. I thought I was being ridiculous, but when I tried to ride away, I couldn't. I had to come back to be sure. And then I saw that you were in trouble and I knew I had to help you."

"But why didn't you tell me all this at first? In the coffee shop?"

"You'd have thought I was crazy. You weren't ready to understand then. I'm not sure you are now."

"I don't understand. You only brought me here because you needed me to play out some role in your myth?"

Johnny is bristling with male defensiveness.

I know I'm on dangerous ground, but I can't seem to help myself. My crutch suddenly feels like rubber. I need so much more from Johnny than this and I thought I had it. If I was wrong, I need to know. I charge on.

"Don't you care about me at all?"

"Dammit woman, of course I care. I admit, the dream brought us together, but you needed me and I needed you."

I am watching, waiting, silently begging him to go on.

He sighs deeply and considers "Okay, at first I thought you were too fragile to take this life, so I tested you. I threw you into the water. I was an idiot and you had every right to march back up the hill and tell me and my spirits to go to hell. But you didn't. You sat there and you enjoyed it. That was when I realized how special you were.

"And then you scared me when you got hypothermia. I almost lost you. But you came back from the land of the dead and fucked my socks off and I knew you were a keeper! You're a gift to me from the spirits. Best gift I ever got. I don't know where all this is leading, but we'll go through it together. We have to trust the spirits."

It's all right. He's made it better. He's mended the sudden tear in my soul. Why do I care what this man or any man thinks of me? I don't know the answer to that. All I know is that I do care what I mean to Johnny. I'm okay for now. My crutch has regained its ability to support my weight.

This vision stuff is all beyond me and a little frightening. It is too big and not my thing at all, but it is Johnny's thing. This is the most important thing in his life and he wants me to be part of it, to contribute. I think that beats the hell out of filling my days with shopping and pastries, waiting for old age.

Johnny knows when I have made my choice. Suddenly, he is impatient. He has other priorities. And I am aware of this also, without a spoken word. It is downright unsettling. I turn to him with an unspoken question.

"I have to report to work today," he explains. "Do you want to come with me?"

"Sure, if I can?..."

"Let's go." He puts out the fire while I consult my purse kit to assess the damage my crying jag has done to my public image. The swollen eyes and blotches are beyond my purse kit's capacity. I shrug and get back on the motorcycle. Johnny takes off with a roar that betrays his impatience. The cycle rides easier without the saddlebags. Johnny is eager, anticipating, and I am curious. What kind of work is it that he goes to so eagerly, and that allows him to take me with him? I am ready for anything after the shock of his camp.

The tide is coming back in. In places it will cover the beach up to the cliffs and we will have to wait until low tide again to come back. I am beginning to understand my new time table.

I take a deep breath of the healing air. I can feel the icy salt-sprayed wind cooling my puffy face. I might look halfway presentable again if the trip takes long enough. The rock formations, the cliffs, the wild dark sea, the gray sand, and the jackstraw tumble of tree trunks bleached by salt water are becoming part of my consciousness. Tame breakers snarl around our wheels. I accept them, and the petty squabbling gulls, the newly scrubbed clouds, and the soft glow of the distant sun. This is my world now and a more beautiful one I could not wish for. It thrills and excites me. I am awake. I am alive. My soul basks in the sunlight and stretches luxuriously. All those years of being cramped in a fetal position are over. I snarl back at the waves. I laugh until the tears threaten to flow again. Outside I soar with the highest gull; inside I am soft wax, melting.

NINE

Rounding a point we enter a long curving inlet set with two large stone islands. The center shore swarms with human activity. I have not seen so many people since we left civilization. Was it only yesterday? I have been listening to the overwhelming stillness of primeval wilderness and the presence of these twenty or so people seems a gross intrusion.

There are houses built on the hillside, an encampment with long, low buildings and a wooden stairway up the bank. But the center of activity seems to be a huge garden-like area. Here people cluster around cells of disturbed earth and around a large wooden comb from which comes a humming noise, that of a power generator, and a constant pumping of water. It all seems casual, but purposeful, not businesslike like a factory, more like a construction site where something is being built. I know what they are doing, but I am disoriented. In another minute I will have it. Fishing? Mining? No.

Johnny parks the bike and we walk over. They are mostly young people, very young. Johnny is welcomed warmly by a size five freckled blonde in short shorts and a halter. She is about my younger daughter's age, and I suddenly remember I have not had a proper bath in twenty-four hours. I reek of last night's fish and wood smoke and lovemaking, and I am not wearing makeup. The girl hustles Johnny off to inspect something and I follow along behind them, aging with every step. We pass a housewifely type in old denims with her hair tied back under a scarf rummaging through a box of rocks with total absorption. This is reassuringly businesslike. I follow Johnny and the sweet young thing to a series of tables fitted with sorting boxes around the edges. Piles of rocks, broken shells, and assorted dirt surround them. The girl picks up a small glass tube with a cork in it, like a test tube, and hands it to Johnny. "Isn't it beautiful? We found it this morning!"

Johnny nods, turning it over and inspecting it carefully. He hands it to me.

Inside the tube is a tiny, exquisitely carved piece of bone with deliberately jagged sides and a pointed tip. Obviously a fishing barb of some kind.

"Elk horn?" Johnny asks the girl.

She nods. "We got nothing but shell fragments all weekend, then this morning, zap, we started getting fire rock and now this. Looks promising."

Johnny moves over to a gray-haired man with thick glasses who sits inspecting rocks with a magnifying glass. The girl and I look at each other. I hand her back the glass tube and smile.

"Beautiful," I say, as though I know what I am talking about.

In a way I am beginning to. Anyone could appreciate the workmanship in the artifact, and I know where we are. It has to be the university archaeological excavation site I read about in the Sunday supplements.

The girl puts the tube away carefully in its rack. "I'm Sheri Hansen," she says. "You official or just visiting?"

"Ruth Kristinsdottir. Unofficial." I like the sound of it. Enigmatic.

"Can I show you around?"

I am not sure how to take her offer. We are sniffing each other warily. "I don't want to interfere with your work," I object.

"No problem. This is my work. I'm a gofer and a guide. My job this week is tours."

"Then by all means, enlighten me."

I look around with satisfaction. So this is a "dig"! I have always wanted to visit one. I have read thrilling accounts of uncovering the past in Egypt, Mycennae, and South Africa. This looks very dull compared to those, but I imagine that all excavation sites are boring most of the time. Unless you have the obsession. This must be Johnny's obsession. The camp certainly fits. No wonder my age did not bother him! He is used to artifacts.

Sheri is moving back toward the grids and beginning her spiel. I hurry to catch up. I do not want to miss any of it.

"This site is special not only because it's old, pre-Columbian, but because the artifacts are so well preserved by the mud slides that covered the village at least twice. The village was continuously occupied up until the turn of the century, when the government forced the parents to move to the present reservation so the children could go to school.

"This is the first house that was excavated. The shell midden, of course, indicated a campsite; that's the accumulation of white shell fragments in the sand, but then a storm washed away part of the bank in front of the house and exposed some of its contents, giving us a head start on excavating the site. This is the oldest and the largest house so far and the richest in artifacts. It was at the bottom so to speak. Others were built above it and to the sides. We have no idea yet how many houses were built in the village. We guess that the center of the village may have been further south, and perhaps the older and richer houses are there. The houses to the north where we are digging now seem to be poorer ones, smaller, less elaborately furnished, and some of them incomplete as though they were 'cannibalized,' if you'll pardon the expression, for newer house building." She giggles nervously at the reference. I resolve to ask Johnny about it.

"Every ounce of dirt is removed carefully," Sheri continues. "This particular dig is noted for the technique we are able to use in removing dirt—by water. We hose down the clay to remove it gently without damaging the fragile artifacts. Almost everything imaginable is preserved in that air-tight clay coating—delicate woven baskets, hair, bone, wood—things that would normally deteriorate in the air. We have to treat them quickly with a paraffin mixture to replace the moisture or they will crumble to dust."

"These mud slides," I ask slowly, "They came quickly and didn't allow people to move things out, or even to escape themselves?"

Sheri changes the subject. "All the artifacts belong to the tribe and are catalogued and displayed in the tribe's museum on the reservation."

"Then these are tombs, literally," I continue.

"You had better ask Johnny about that. I'm not allowed to discuss it. I see a group has gathered. I have to go do a regular tour. You're welcome to come along if you like."

Sheri moves away hurriedly. This is something else I shall have to ask Johnny about, later.

Johnny has been watching me covertly from over the diagrams he has supposedly been studying. I ignore him. He is playing another one of his mind reading games. It comes from too much reliance on telepathic communication. This whole experience is too vast for me to absorb at once. There is more than the key to a lost culture buried under all this mud. At least for Johnny, and I suspect for me as well. I decide that my soul is too impatient to ever be an archaeologist. The sheer magnitude of the job they are doing to get such small rewards depresses me. They are measuring, charting, cleaning, sorting, boxing, and labeling thousands of pounds of sand, rock, and shell fragments, literally peeling back the layers of earth an inch at a time. I am prone to rip open wrapped packages to get at the present inside. I always eat the candy first for fear I might not be hungry later or that someone might get it before I do. I would never be able to wait years to start digging at the center where I know all the good stuff is. I would have started there.

It often amazes me that someone as impatient as I am could have postponed my life for twenty years. I have an awful lot of making up to do. I must have suffered from it. I could not have gotten off easily; there has to be more damage than shows on the surface. Hard to assess though, until all the folds are out of my wings and they have dried enough to test. They might crumble into dust from disuse and drop me into the sea.

What happens to things cocooned for twenty years? Physical things dry out, deteriorate like those artifacts they are digging out of the bank. And what about the soul? Talents, emotions, skills, potential? Skills have to be used and developed to survive. People dry up and wither away. I have seen them myself. Could I be only a mummy inside, then; a relic to be preserved in a glass case away from the air to keep me from becoming a heap of ashes? Better ashes than an eternal fetus in a jar of formaldehyde, only a germ of what might have been.

Life out here with Johnny will determine how much strength is left in my wings, and damned quickly. If it is too much for me I will soon go screaming back to comfort and safety. We will see how sick my soul is. Do I hear commitment in my tone?

Sheri has vanished. I drift away, trying to find my own significance in the endless nit-picking around me. After all, an archaeological dig is a suitable place for a relic like me to start finding myself.

Johnny joins me before I can go far. I confront him.

"What do you do here?" I ask.

"I'm the tribe's representative on the site. I keep track of what's found because it belongs to the tribe, and I help identify the material for the university, determine what it was and how it was used. I'm kind of a translator.

"I get more out of this job than anybody. I am paid to search for my own ancestors, and I get material and credit toward my doctoral dissertation."

"Then your camp is your laboratory, where you test out theories about how it all worked?"

"Yes, but it's more like drawing a picture of something from a description, making the real thing, using it. Connecting the dots. Taking the dead and breathing life into them. I use the memories of the old people from my tribe to help fill in as much as possible. There are many gaps."

We stand leaning over an excavation, watching the young man in the hole casually hosing away several hundred years of concealment. I am acutely uncomfortable. Disquiet has been edging into my consciousness since we arrived, but I have been dismissing it as the strangeness of the experience. Now I realize it is more. It has become overwhelming. I have to get away, to get out of here. Now!

It is too late. I take a deep breath and suddenly I am choking. I cannot breathe. What is it? I struggle and then I panic. This is deadly serious! Is this it for me? Johnny? Help me! Is it going to be over? Not here, not now! I am choking to death, and at the same time I can see the whole scene clearly. The young man in the hole stands staring, open mouthed, the hose in his hand forgotten. Johnny is frantically pounding me on the back, yelling his frustration at not being able to help. I have to communicate with him.

I point, down into the hole. Johnny understands. He pulls me back, away from the edge of the hole, and then quickly out of the area. I am back in my body, fighting for air, getting an occasional breath now. I am going to be all right. Johnny hurries me down the steps to the beach. We sit on a log as I recover myself in the salt air. A dense fog is packing around the rocks. I shiver watching it, still gasping for control.

"What was it, Ruth?"

"I should ask you!" Talking is not easy yet.

He thinks about it. Do I sense guilt? God help me.

"Johnny?!!"

"Was it some kind of gas that you inhaled; something you could be allergic to?"

I just stare at him.

"No. I thought not. But I had to ask."

I am waiting. I can tell that he does know. His response is maddeningly slow, reluctant. "It has happened to me, but not that violently. I need to know exactly what you felt. Several times I have had to run, to get away. The feeling is overpowering. Nausea, terror, I don't know. But it shouldn't have affected you. It doesn't seem to bother any of them," his gesture includes the encampment.

"Well, it got me. It was all that, what you said, and worse. Johnny, I couldn't breathe! My face was covered, I was smothering; my mouth and nose and eyes felt full of dirt, sand, something?... What was it?"

"Maybe it wasn't such a good idea to bring you here."

"I am here. That's not an answer. You know what it is, I know you do. Tell me what is going on!"

"We have a belief in our tribe, about the dead. If they are not properly sent off into the next world, their spirits remain trapped with their bodies. If someone drowns, and his body is not recovered, his spirit must live in the sea. That place where it is imprisoned is a bad place. Things happen there."

"And if the person is buried alive in a mud slide, his spirit remains trapped with him." Now I am understanding.

"You felt it. Did it feel like something free, released, at peace?"

"Hardly. So that's what you are really doing here! Freeing the dead's lost spirits."

"Yes. I'm sorry you got pulled into that part of it."

"I almost got pulled into the other world! I could have died. I could have choked to death if you hadn't pulled me out of there. Johnny? Could that really have happened?"

"I don't know. I don't think so. But I can't be sure. I can't guarantee you are going to survive this if you stay. Obviously you have an even bigger role in my drama than I dreamed."

"Thanks a lot. I'm sure I'm not going to stick around here with these grave robbers, anyway."

"They're not that at all. They are freeing the trapped spirits of the dead, finding them and allowing a proper burial."

"But they're not allowed to talk about it? Sheri wouldn't answer my questions."

"They all sign an agreement not to."

"Why make a mystery of it? Why not just tell people the problem you have?"

"Because they won't understand. What would your reaction have been if you hadn't felt the spirit yourself? Would you believe it possible or would you dismiss it as some savage superstition, a stupid old wives' tale? You non-Indians believe that the spirit is totally free of the body after death. This is important and personal to us. We don't want it discounted like everything else about our beliefs. And there's more to it than that. We also believe that if you speak of the dead, remember them, even think about them, you call them back."

"Well, I certainly did do that, when I asked Sheri about what happened to the people."

"So I guess that's something else you won't dismiss as superstition."

"Superstition?!" I retort. "A boogey word thought up by some overzealous early Christian. That word alone has put man's understanding of himself back about two-thousand years. I do understand! This may sound silly, but I had a cat once that I was very attached to, more than I was to most of the humans in my life. He had a soul, this cat, an old, beautiful soul. When he died I very quietly opened the door to let that soul go outside. And I buried him outdoors. It seemed like the thing to do. But I don't tell anybody that."

Johnny hugs me. "I knew your instincts were sound. I believe you are basically a pagan. We'll find out soon."

"If I survive."

"Right. I'm going to catch some lunch. That's something I can understand and do something about. Build a fire and try to stay in this dimension for a few minutes until I get back."

My laugh is shaky and I watch him leave, with deep reluctance, as he disappears into the fog and the swirling tide flow, as though he had never been. The emptiness he leaves is a deep dark hole. A cold one. I shiver beside it, then busy myself gathering firewood. I will have to learn to build a fire without a match as Johnny does, if I am to fully participate. My role is defined—pre-Columbian squaw. How is that going to help me learn to fly? I suspect I will have to crawl a ways first.

Johnny is gone maybe twenty minutes, just long enough for me to become alarmed. My nerves are stretched past tolerance. I am raw, edgy, hyper. Finally, when I feel about to scream he appears out of the fog, bearing two large crabs. He hands them to me, claws waving, kisses me gently, gestures for me to wait, and then disappears up the staircase to the university camp quarters. I sit down holding the crabs at arms' length until he reappears with a medium-sized watertight basket. He fills it with fresh water. I toss the crabs into the basket of water and stalk off into the fog to cry.

In a little while Johnny comes to get me. "Lunch is ready," he says gently.

"I couldn't bear to watch you boil them alive."

"I'll tell you a secret. I don't. I split them first. They don't feel a thing. I never could stand to watch them swimming around as the water got hot. It takes forever to heat up with the fire rocks. Don't tell on me."

What do you do with a man like that? You grab him. He dodges and races me back to the fire. The crab is in no danger of being over-cooked. Fortunately, crab needs little cooking. I imagine Johnny's ancestors ate a lot of rare meat. I mention it.

"A lot of it was smoked. Very well done, dried out tough as leather. Fish, shellfish, meat, berries, seaweed, you name it, with and without fish roe, and all dipped in seal or whale oil. Lots of seal and whale oil."

"Yuck!"

"You'll learn to love it. The perfume!"

I groan. Then it hits me. "You haven't got either whale or seal oil! You can't kill either one of them!"

He laughs and pulls my braids. "Candlefish have lots of oil in them. The oil helps preserve the meat without refrigeration."

"I don't believe you have that either."

"To be honest, I never could acquire a taste for it. And I don't know anyone on the res, even among the old folks, who likes fish oil anymore. Terrible to think you can change a thousand-year-old taste preference in two generations. How much else have we lost?"

"But fish oil!"

"You non-Indians pour oil all over salads and fry things in it and put butter on everything else. Ours tasted a little fishier is all, like anchovies, an acquired taste."

Lunch is over. Johnny announces he is going back to work.

"I've got to get *something* done today. You'll be all right. I can send Sheri down to keep you company?"

"No thanks. What did you tell them up there, anyway? Did they ask about me?"

"Sure. I told them you were subject to fits!"

He departs hastily on this exit line, leaving me to clean up the mess, which is easy given the biodegradable nature of our picnic. He took the cooking basket back with him.

In spite of the normality of my task, a sense of the unreal continues to muffle the afternoon. If I felt even a little acclimated before,

I have lost that foothold. I can see no further than the fog permits. Somewhere above me the sun shines. At sea level, the fog advances and retreats capriciously.

As much as I want to be with Johnny, I would rather be alone than join them all up there on the bank at their macabre task. I have not until now thought of archeology as ghoulish. But I have never thought of the "before," only the dusty "after." Archaeology always seemed to be a dry, scientific, treasure hunt. Until this morning.

Real people died there, many of them, and died horribly, smothering where they slept; mothers, children, and perhaps a warrior or two, but mostly the young, because there would be few old people. Life expectancy was short. They were buried under tons of mud. The lucky ones would have been knocked unconscious first by falling house beams before the onslaught of mud covered them. But some must have lived long enough to know their fate. I have glimpsed that moment. And I relive it thinking about the dig. I must force myself to think of something else, or I could bring them back!

Think of what? I have a problem here. I have no past. I have cut myself off from my former life. Thoughts of it have no relevance here. And I have too little experience of my new life to fall back on it for distraction. I am a newborn. Johnny, I must think of Johnny, of his touch. Tide is almost out. Soon we can go back to camp, back to a longhouse just like the ones under the mud. Jesus. I *have* to think of something else.

Pagan. Johnny called me a pagan. It is true. My father taught me to worship Truth above all else, and I believed him. But I lived happily in the Christian tradition until one day when I was nineteen. That day I said some magic words: "The world is much easier to understand without metaphysics." The words were barely spoken when the heavens split open with doubt and the next moment I stood irrevocably on the other side of belief staring back at a tradition to which I could never return.

That day is as significant in my life as if it were yesterday. And it served the same function, to separate me dramatically from one segment of my life and throw me headlong into the next. I do not make changes gently, logically. I suppose I will approach my death as violently.

Johnny is standing over me. I seem to have begun whimpering.

"Ruth? What am I going to do with you?" I smile up at him sheepishly. "Sorry. I can't seem to help it. Johnny? Look directly behind you and to your left, by that stunted pine."

"What stunted pine? There isn't one within sight of us."

"About four or five yards away, just at the top of the hill. There is no pine tree? Nobody standing under it?"

"I see a number of people by that rock out near the water's edge, and a couple peering over the bank from the top of the staircase, but that is absolutely all. Ruth, have you ever been . . . sensitive?"

"Never! Not in the way you mean. You're telling me there is no tree and no one standing under it? When can we go home?"

"How far home?"

"To your camp. I told you I can't go back to my old life."

"You've got guts. Maybe more than I have. What do you see over there?"

"Nothing. Obviously. Since there is nothing there, I see no one. There was someone there. Once. And a tree. A trick of the light, of the fog. When can we leave here?"

"Now. I'll get my gear and meet you at the motorcycle. Unless you'd rather come with me?"

"No. Not up there. *They* aren't here. Where I am. *They* are up there. All of them. And I want no part of it."

Johnny hurries. I sit, huddled, focusing on the bit of sand in front of me. It, at least, remains what it is; it is of this time and place. What is happening to me?

I don't remember ever having paranormal experiences before. I have always accepted the possibility of them; real, physical phenomena that come from an also real sixth sense, none of which are recognized by the scientific community.

I have even come to accept the possibility of another dimension, as immediate and personal as this one, and the possibility of communication of some sort between the two through the sixth sense. I have no trouble reconciling these beliefs with my rejection at nineteen of Protestant metaphysics and its self-serving version of heaven and God. Metaphysics is beyond the physical. This is not beyond the physical. I am feeling it right here and now.

Johnny is right. I *am* a pagan. No wonder I am fitting so neatly into the world of his past. And then suddenly, a memory surfaces, from perhaps six or seven years ago. Richard and I were on vacation one summer at a ranch in eastern Colorado, in the heart of Anasazi territory. The ranch had a number of ruins on the property, including two kivas, or temples.

I was mercifully alone. Richard and the children had gone on a hike. I walked up to the small kiva. As I started up the path, I noticed that something strange was happening to my perception. I seemed to be walking through time. The afternoon heat was heavy with a strange soup of energies and I displaced them as I passed.

It was the summer solstice and I was tracing an ancient path in the company of a crowd of celebrants. We were to perform a ritual. I walked purposefully and prayerfully with the rest.

At the top of the mound, I found a ladder leading down through the entrance, or smoke hole, into the dark ground. I climbed down with the others. Inside the circular structure, the only light came from the opening above us and, oddly, from a small ceremonial fire in the center of the structure. One part of my mind knew that the fire had not burned there for hundreds of years. but its glow lit this room now, flickering shadows on the walls, which I feared to look at too closely.

A voice instructed me to walk slowly around the fire counter-clockwise, winding time backward with each step. There was a chant now, and a drumbeat, which echoed the beating of my heart. I did not know the words of the chant but I became part of them. I was carried along in a stream of energy without any effort on my part. I was powerless to stop the movement and I did not try. I gave myself wholly to the experience. It felt right; warm, peaceful, and fulfilling, in a way that was new to me. We moved back and further back to the Beginning.

"Now kneel," the voice commanded. I knelt to find myself before a small depression in the earth, which the architect supervising the excavation of the ruins had explained was the sipapu, the opening to the earth's womb from which man had emerged. Make the offering came the directive. I reached into the pouch that I seemed to be carrying. and brought out a tiny decorated clay vessel that held corn pollen. I placed some of the corn pollen into the sipapu.

"We are pleased," the voice continued, "Now rise and return as you have come."

I circled the fire pit slowly, clockwise this time, to the beat of the drum, still borne by the energy of my unearthly companions, back through the years to the foot of the ladder and out of the dimness of the kiva into the light of the afternoon.

I moved on down the path to the present. My companions fell away as I walked.

Finally the path came to an end. I stopped. The voice said, "You will remember this only when the time is right. Your mate will lead you then where you need to go. You have done well my daughter. You need never be afraid. You are not alone."

I walked slowly back to the ranch house hugging my feeling of being greatly blessed, and as was foretold, I never thought of the experience again until now. Now I am drawing comfort from the memory and its promise. I am, it seems, after all, the woman from Johnny's dream, and I am to follow where he leads me.

Johnny has returned. He leads me to his motorcycle. I can only imagine what he has told the others, but we have quite an audience as we ride away. It is a most chauvinistic exit; I feel like chattel stashed on the back of the motorcycle. I feel the eyes of those liberated women on my back, and there is envy in them. Any one of them would gladly trade places with me! I know I have a prize. I hug his back. I see a lot of Johnny's back, but it is undeniably a nice back.

It is in fact one of the great backs of all time. I can not envision a greater one. The relief, the release of tension I feel moving out of sight of the inlet acts as an aphrodisiac. As usual, Johnny senses my mood. He lifts one of my hands to his lips and kisses it slowly, then bites it playfully. The rest of the ride passes in a haze of desire. I feel none of the cold exhilaration of the first trip. But it seems longer because I am impatient. I am, in fact, uncomfortable. I ache for him. I am dripping with moisture, turned inside out with lust.

We go directly inside when we get to camp. No conversation is necessary. We have total agreement on the chief priority. Johnny, too, is in a hurry. He tries a few short cuts. It does not matter. I am gone. Off. Into the ecstasy that mimics agony.

TEN

"How would you like to go elk hunting?"

Johnny is sitting on the edge of the sleeping platform watching me, apparently completely recovered from our orgy.

"Me? I thought that was men's work."

"I could use your help. I saw a young bull day before yesterday while we were hiking. It's rare for one to come down this far from the mountains, especially in the summer. We might as well have some fresh meat. If I do it by myself it'll take me two days. But both of us might make it back by tonight."

I sigh. I can see the sun shining through the doorway. Yesterday's fog belongs to yesterday. Trekking in the woods with Johnny will be preferable to the excavation. Besides, he has used an irresistible plea. He needs me. I sigh again, knowing I will regret it. "When?"

"Now. Get dressed."

"Bring me some coffee and I'll get up fast enough!" I am almost too limp to move. For someone who is supposed to be learning to walk alone, I am certainly enjoying my crutch! Sex is a great aid in adjusting to unusual sleeping arrangements. I recommend it. The hard wooden bench has seemed quite comfortable. Dressing is impossibly difficult. It involves moving around. Johnny, who is already dressed, watches me, frowning. He starts to peel off his clothes.

"What are you doing? I thought we were going hunting?"

"I've got to speed you up. Forget the clothes. Come on."

He grabs my hands and pulls me out into the sunlit morning. We run through the wind into the surf. One plunge into the icy salt water does it. Adrenaline roars through my veins. I race back to the shelter of the house and my warm clothes, laughing and cursing and loving the excitement of the forbidden. Nude bathing in broad daylight! I can imagine Richard's face. Or my mother's! I feel free. Cold, but free. Wild and wantonly free. A sob catches in my throat. If it were all to end in the next few minutes, at least I have had this. I have not felt this young since I was this young; sixteen, seventeen maybe. It is glorious. It is incredible. The forty-two-year-old in me knows it cannot happen and is afraid. I cherish the moment all the more because of its brevity. I hide my tears in my shirt, not wanting or able to explain. Johnny has already given me so much. More than any man I have known since my father.

We take the cycle back up the dwindling beach toward our first night's camp. Again, contrite, I realize Johnny's hurry was to catch the tide. I wonder if I will ever become acclimated enough to operate on that clock. Riding until the foam blows around our tires, Johnny finally has to stop before the backwash catches us. We have run out of dry beach. Johnny stashes the motorcycle behind some rocks and we climb the bluff and take off through the woods.

Sunlight has withdrawn to the tops of the trees. We climb steadily through new-growth pine, pushing our way through heavy under-brush. The earth is black under the pine needles, with the scars of an old burn. The air is full of the sound of my own heavy breathing.

"We haven't been here before," I protest with difficulty. "How do you know this elk is here?"

"We have an appointment with him."

He is kidding. Or is he? Johnny traces his own pattern, and I have no option except to follow him and do as I am told. The elk and I are both part of Johnny's game plan. He defines the rules and we must abide by them.

This frees me. Frees us both, the elk and me, of responsibility. Of choice. My role is reversed now. Just recently I felt hunted; now I am hunter. The world is redefined. All my senses are heightened, not dulled by other preoccupations that discount them. I feel the soft still air caress my skin, see the crystalline light define each leaf distinctly from its brother leaf, hear the leaves sigh and breathe and grow, smell the pungent dampness, taste the salt sweat on my lips.

We are no longer climbing steeply but seem to have angled off along a ridge. We follow an old, distinct animal path which leads through a grove of giant trees spared by the fire. Their greedy roots weed out the undergrowth, creating a hushed park. Soaring hemlocks whisper among themselves, conferring about the stranger who passes below.

I wish for protective coloring like the fat slugs, greenish here, indistinct against the foliage. The sun is remotely benevolent, its filtered light has lost its warmth along with its brightness. Countless tiny streams trickle past under the tree roots and rotted logs, only their tiny music betraying their presence.

It is a magical place and not a safe one. The cry of a hunting bird sounds over head. Insects scurry for cover. Every shadow is a hiding place for victim and for predator. The deceptive calm will flare momentarily with violence and then resume its rhythm; one life taken, another sustained.

"Who are you who come seeking the elk?"

The voice, deep, ancient, is a sibilant sigh on the wind. The Elders, the giant hemlocks surrounding me, wait for my reply.

The answer lies buried deep within me, if only I can reach it . . . I stretch to my limits and beyond and then I know what it is they want from me.

"My mother was hunger, my father was fear. I am one of the free. I am animal." Over head the giants sigh. The verdict passes. I am accepted; I belong.

Magically, my breathing eases. My lungs suddenly expand, strong from use, able to carry me swiftly from danger on the steepest oxygen-scarce slope. I shift my powerful body easily on four sturdy graceful legs. I am the elk, testing the wind for a hint of predator. I shy at a falling leaf, skittish in this morning with the scent of my blood on it. I place my dainty hooves carefully on the path, leaving a sharp, beautiful print in the earth, softened where a mole has disturbed it.

Johnny is smiling to himself. I cannot see his face, but I feel his smile. He knows I am an elk following him, stalking him. It amuses him. I wonder what would happen if Johnny should turn now and not recognize me, see only the elk and kill me. Would I die trapped in the elk's body? The thought frightens me. In that moment the elk is gone and I am a woman, city soft and panting with exertion on the hill.

"Damn," I say. Johnny laughs softly. He knows. Was it a trick of my imagining? Or did it happen? I look back and then search quickly on the path behind us. There, where I placed my hoof in the soft dirt of the mole's digging, is a sharp, clear hoof print. I look up. Johnny is standing beside me.

"It did happen," I say with awe.

"Trust it. Trust yourself."

"But how could it be?"

"This is my world, not yours. In your world it isn't possible. Your world rejects everything it cannot see or touch. The eye sees very little of the riches that surround us.

"My tribe's legends tell of a time when all creatures—human, animal, fish, and bird—could exchange forms easily. To be able to do so today is a mark of special favor by the spirits.

"Come, we have a date with an elk. Your mate. And no talking. From now on we must be quiet."

I walk along behind him. I am part of it all now in spite of myself, in spite of my heritage. My choice to follow him has brought me here, involved me in something I do not understand. What have I done? What has just happened to me? How was it done? Can I do it again? Do I want to do it again?

First, yesterday's suffocation horror and now this. It is coming too fast. Moments of ecstasy and power, of beauty and terror kaleidoscope crazily, as though the air were full of a hallucinogen. His world and not mine. Unquestionably. But what is it that makes it different? I could have walked with Richard through these woods in my old life and seen nothing but trees, felt nothing but discomfort.

Pain in my stomach reminds me that I have not eaten since . . . When? Lunch yesterday! Soon it will be twenty-four hours. I am ravenous. I whimper slightly, involuntarily, at the violence of my hunger.

"Hunt on an empty stomach," Johnny hisses. "You're fasting."

Some sort of religious rite, no doubt. I will believe anything today. Hunger will pass. There are more vital concerns ahead, of that I am certain.

We are climbing again, even more steeply than before. I try to use the elk trick again to ease my labored breathing, but now it does not work. When I really need it, it won't happen.

Eating is not to be taken for granted in Johnny's world. It takes a lot of work. There are no supermarkets or kitchen appliances to help us forget where the food came from. We have to hike miles uphill to catch today's only meal. He is going to taste very good, that elk, no matter how tough or poorly cooked. And if he should get away? We go hungry. Or pull our tired bodies together and go fishing again. In the dark? Can you catch fish or shellfish in the dark? Do they sleep? But Johnny will not miss. I feel sorry for this elk. He is as good as dead. I have an almost superstitious respect for Johnny's abilities.

We come to a halt on a steep slope. Sheer rock walls climb one side, on the other the hill drops away beyond a deep crevasse formed when part of the cliff crumbled and eroded to a finger of granite. Johnny stations me at the lower end of the crevasse in the middle of the narrow path with a curious bone whistle.

"Blow on this for awhile, not steadily, but at intervals. The elk will come down the path in front of you. The wind is with him so he won't spot you until he comes around that bend. He'll be curious about the whistle. Keep blowing softly, even when you see him. Don't look directly at him, look away as though you don't see him or care about his presence. If he should try to bolt past you, yell and wave your arms and make a racket to scare him."

Johnny disappears down the path in the direction we have just come, which I find curious. I settle down to wait, glad for the rest, but with mixed emotions about the proposed trap. I feel guilty about being a siren, piping the poor elk to his death. I must concentrate on how hungry I am and start blowing.

The whistle sounds lonely and alien in the silence of the morning. Without the shelter of trees, the sun is hot on the dirt of the path and on my head. It feels good. The whistle has only one note but I can vary it with wind pressure. I feel self-conscious about sitting here blowing away, all by myself.

Suppose something other than the elk should come down the path? Where would I go? The clever trap would catch me instead of the elk. A bear, perhaps, or a cougar? Fortunately, Johnny is out there somewhere to rescue me, but what if he is too far away to hear me scream? I have felt my death on the wind, but was it for me as an elk or as a human? Surely Johnny would not make a mistake like that. If there were any danger for me he would know about it. I think. But he is human after all.

What is human and what is more than human, superhuman? The lines are beginning to blur. What I have seen and done seem natural and human because they happened to me. But they came from a source within me that I did not dream existed.

The wind blows damp and cold down the natural draw, from the direction the elk will come. It sends shivers down my spine in spite of the hot sun overhead. It must be just after noon. Waiting is hard. I hope Johnny is quick; I do not want to have to watch. I have never seen anything that large die. I watched my mother kill chickens when I was quite small. On my grandfather's farm it was the ritual that when company drove up somebody would run out back to kill a chicken for dinner. My mother would wring its neck and chop off its head. Sometimes the bird got away and flopped around headless until she caught it again and plunged it into the waiting bucket of boiling water. I recall having no emotion about it other than fascination. It is hard to become attached to chickens, especially on a working farm. Children accept their elders' attitudes toward violence.

But I have become old and squeamish, sheltered by sanitary supermarkets from the bloody necessities of butchering. I shudder now when I drive past feedlots where hundreds of cattle wait their turn to die. This is better. The elk is free, up until the moment his fate becomes linked with ours.

I continue to blow on the whistle. I wait, tensed on the sun-hot path, long past tolerance. Expectation has dwindled into anticlimax when I look up to see the elk coming down the path toward me. I startle and stare until I remember Johnny's instructions. I look away and blow softly on the whistle. He is large, a drab and velvety creature with new horns. I can just see him on the periphery of my vision. He hesitates, weighing menace against curiosity. My heart wants to cry out to him to flee, but it is too late. Johnny is on the path behind him.

I am on my feet transfixed. The moment is set, like a frieze in bronze, a triangle of two human figures, male and female, and the elk. The elk rears, cornered, and turns, his back hooves slipping as the crumbling earth gives way beneath him, lowering him into the intended trap. Then he is in the crevasse, neck high, straining to release himself. Johnny hands me a club.

"Kill him," he says. His eyes are black crystals. I am mute, stunned.

"Kill him," he repeats.

"I can't," I beg.

"You are hungry. Kill him or never eat meat again," he hisses.

I hate him. How can he make me do this? I have been the elk, how can I kill him? Johnny's voice is relentless.

"You can't ask others to do your killing for you. Do it, and do it fast. It's cruel to make him wait. He knows it's coming and he is suffering. Do it now!"

It is true. The elk has stopped thrashing around. He is staring at me with wide, terrified eyes. He knows.

Johnny continues, "Behind the horns. Stun him. Quickly."

I take a deep breath and shut my heart to pity. I bring the club down on the back of his neck with all my strength just as he rears again. My arms are wrenched almost out of their sockets. Johnny takes the club and strikes him again. The elk staggers and goes down. Johnny hands me his knife.

"Finish it! Cut his throat so he will bleed. It's painless."

I jump into the pit beside the fallen animal. His eyes are glazed. I have to get it over with before I am sick. The frieze has changed. Instead of three figures there are now two, the elk and me, and the knife in my hand forms the triangle. It is a blood rite, a sacrifice. The elk, victim, will be transformed, his life on this earth ended so that his flesh will nourish my flesh. Gone is the personalized sense of revulsion. I am an impersonal agent of fate. It is a moment of deep solemnity, of reverence, of appreciation of life at the moment of death. The elk is dead, long live the elk.

I draw the knife across the elk's throat almost with a flourish, wanting to send him off in style. If he has to die, it will not be carelessly or heedlessly. I have cut the artery. His blood pours out over me. I cry. I climb out of the hole and stand sobbing quietly, profoundly moved by his death at my hand.

Once again there is a deep sigh of satisfaction, which does not come from Johnny. I can feel his approval separately, near me. This approval comes from all around me, from the rocks, from the wind, from the sun's warmth flowing about my head. I have passed another test, come a little closer to understanding.

Johnny is dressing the carcass more rapidly than I would have thought possible. Soon it is just a piece of meat on the hoof. A dead thing. Curious.

I stop crying. "You ordered me to kill coldbloodedly," I comment.

"There was no other way. If you'd had time to think about it, you'd have rationalized yourself out of it. You just had to trust me."

"Did you plan this all along?"

He shrugs. "It worked out. It was something you needed to do."

"Yes." I look at the bloody carcass, now headless, legless, and disemboweled. "It was the right thing to do. I'm not sure why, but it was."

"He's going to taste awfully good instead of fish." Johnny is rigging a pulley to haul the meat out of the hole. "Here, put your weight on this," he says. Together we raise the carcass and swing it out of the crevasse. Johnny unearths a small pole from behind the rocks and tips it down into the hole. "Small animals will have a feast. Wouldn't want them to get trapped."

I stand looking at the remains of the elk. It seems enormous. Even dressed it must weigh 250 to 300 pounds.

"Closer to 350," Johnny says, reading my mind again. He wraps the body with crude ropes of twisted bark. He must have brought them with him, but I did not notice him carrying them.

"How are we going to get that heavy thing back to camp?" I ask suspiciously.

He looks at me with speculation. "That depends. That's why I brought you along. We can either drag it with headbands, or we could move it, Indian style."

"How?"

"In the old days, the body would follow the hunter home."

"What?!"

"I've tried, but I've never been successful in persuading a carcass to do that. I thought maybe you . . . Anyway, if nothing better happens, it's easier to drag with two people pulling."

"Let me understand this. We're supposed to 'persuade' a lifeless, headless, gutless corpse to follow us maybe five miles home?"

"It's downhill most of the way."

I am laughing, amused but not amazed. I know I would not have believed it possible the day before yesterday. But today? . . .

"How do you suggest we begin this miracle?" I ask.

"I have no idea. There are no directions."

"I vote we attach headbands to the ropes and start pulling and hope for the best."

He nods and we begin. We give one big heave and the carcass moves only lightly. I gasp.

"Wait a minute. I have changed my mind. This deserves more consideration. Concentrate. We must concentrate on lifting the weight of the corpse off the ground. A song. We need a song. Isn't that the way it's done?"

"Of course! The spirit of the elk is here, with us still. We ask him politely to walk himself home behind us." Johnny begins haltingly to chant in a language he knows only secondhand. I try to repeat what he is saying, thinking hard, willing the thing to happen. We pull. The elk does not move.

I signal Johnny to continue his chant while I think. Or rather feel and listen. I take in the rarity of the day's momentousness. A fly buzzes loudly, circling us, attracted by the scent of blood. I am inside the afternoon, a part of the sun's heat, the elk's blood spilt on the crumbling yellow clay, and part of the fly's journey.

I place my hands on the still warm, hair-covered flank, and feel the flesh beneath the hide. Some of the hairs are sticky with blood. It comes away on my fingers. I taste it. It is salty, cloyingly rich, strong. I am bathed in the elk's blood. This animal is now part of me and moves with me. I am part of him. We move as one.

With my hands touching the elk's flank, I move slowly backwards on the path. The elk is still with me. Cautiously, hardly daring to breathe for fear of breaking the frail but steady flow of energy linking us, I move down the path, the elk not seeming to move, although still attached to my hands. He is with me. Slowly, carefully, I turn sideways, not moving my hands, and walk normally down the path, my hands to one side, resting firmly as before on the elk's carcass.

I gather strength and exaltation as I move. Johnny slips ahead of me to guide my steps, but he need not bother. I move down a path that has opened for me, and nothing and no one will impede me. I have an appointment to keep. The elk is my guide and he has gone before to guide me.

We float, the three of us, effortlessly back to the beach where we left the bike. Johnny attaches the ropes around the carcass to the back of the cycle and we try pulling it, Johnny chanting as before, but it is no use. The machine has spoiled it. I have lost contact. We drag a heavy, unwieldy dead thing, straining the motor to pull it in the sand, catching it on rocks and driftwood and having to stop to free it, wrestling the beast the rest of the way home. We arrive late, after dark, a pair of bloody hunters home with the kill.

ELEVEN

Johnny is gone when I wake. The first thing I see when I open my eyes is the carcass of the elk hanging from a roof beam in the middle of the room. Stuck in it where I will not miss it is Johnny's knife. I laugh out loud at his sign language. "Here's your tool, woman, go to work," it says.

I am being tested again. But this time I am at least in a dimension where the ground rules are familiar. Housekeeping or longhouse-keeping, even cavekeeping has changed a lot in the last several million years, but the principles surely have not. It is an ancient profession, dating back to a time when the first division of labor sent men out to hunt and left the women to tend the fire and the children. In exchange for her services she was provided for by her man. Women are still bartering themselves for that kind of security.

Right. I have a lot of work to do. And no coffee. Drastic measures are called for. I check out the territory and run naked across the beach into the surf. I come out knowing I am forty-two-years old. But I am awake. Boy, am I awake. And cold. And reeking of wood smoke, coated with a film of grease and charcoal and trapped dirt and blood. The cold salt water will not touch any of it. I look at my clothes. They are stiff with the same mess. I look like a test case for a laundry commercial. Could any detergent get this clean? If only I had any detergent.

The next shock of the day is that the fire is cold. A mild panic grips me. All I need to make my morning is to have to start a fire with two sticks! Frantically, I search the ashes for a live ember. My panic is mounting. I do not think I can do it. I am not ready. The day will be shot without a fire. Finished before I begin. Hurrah! An ember. I tenderly feed it, fan it, and nurse it through its infancy into a full blown adolescence. Like most adolescents, it is sulky and disinclined to cooperate.

There's not much firewood. My first priority today will be feeding the fire. I am ravenous. I approach the hanging carcass hesitantly, then grasp the knife and hack out a rib that I suspend over the smoky fire between the two forked sticks we used the night before for cooking. While the meat cooks I assess the situation. First I need firewood. Problem two is preserving the meat. Even considering the chill factor from the wind, in the summer warmth it is going to spoil rapidly. I have to be faster than the bacteria and they have a whole night's head start on me. There is also the matter of the pelt, or what's left of the hide after having been dragged through the sand behind the bike. I am determined to save it. And then there is a dinner to prepare for Johnny. Traditional, expected, and I am determined that he will be pleased by what I have accomplished in his absence.

The goals are clear, but how a former middle-class housewife with no electricity is going to accomplish them is another matter. I know nothing about drying meat. Or curing animal skins. All I have is a reluctant fire, some skeletal wooden fish drying racks outside, and a knife. I always wondered how I would have measured up in the wilderness, how I would have coped with the necessities. This is my opportunity to find out.

And then of course, there is my own personal and immediate goal of getting clean. Johnny does not believe in buying soap, of that I am certain. I cannot imagine how you get clean without it. I suspect you do not. Cleanliness is a relative condition, anyway; it depends on the eye of the beholder, or how tired she may be. Pounding clothes with a stick in running cold water does not seem very efficient. I assume there are certain plants that will produce some small sudsing action to cut grease, but I do not have them. Boiling the clothes will help, except for the wool jacket, and elbow grease is always good, but if I could manage to make some soap. . . . I have never tried soapmaking, but I have read descriptions of it somewhere, and I can at least try. That is, I could if I had a kettle. All I have are two watertight boiling baskets and a pile of fire rocks. Those will have to do. I will need grease or fat, and lye, which is made somehow from wood ashes. There are plenty of both in the raw. I will have to "try" or "fry" down the animal fat. That is what I need the kettle (my basket) for. I can cut off all the fat, boil it, and skim it off the top of the water instead of frying it. That should work. I can also use the pot of water for making soup out of the bones and trimmings from my butchering. Now, that is a first, positive, planning step. I am pleased with myself.

As for the preserving of the meat, I am at a loss. I have canned in sterilized jars (I have none), and I have frozen various kinds of foods (I have no freezer). I have smoked roasts and chickens in the rotisserie on our patio, but that is poor training for the task ahead. Besides, smoking retards spoilage for a short period, but not for very long by itself. Salt, is what I need. But I have none, and I am beginning to miss it. There is always the sea. It must be possible to leave pans of sea water out in the sun for several days and harvest salt. I wonder if it would be edible? By the time I had enough, the meat would probably be spoiled but I would have some for the next time. I shall have to try it, in my spare time, of course.

Air or sun drying takes forever, I am sure, especially in this climate. The combination of drying and smoking must be what you do with the drying racks. There are ashes under them from old, smoking fires. Okay, I think maybe I can handle that. Three basic procedures: boiling, smoking, and making salt. No, four; I forgot the pelt. Then there is making of soap. Five. Now we are getting somewhere. I have a game plan.

First things first. Firewood. Out into the brush I go with my trusty stone hatchet. Johnny's hatchet. I will need regular firewood, and alder, probably green alder for the smoking fires. First, I'll have to get enough regular firewood to keep the cooking fire going while I find the rest of the wood. There is plenty of old driftwood and deadwood around for firewood without cutting any. Even a clumsy tenderfoot like myself can drag an old log home. But cutting green alder is another matter. By the time I get a small pile of it, my cooking fire has burned dangerously low.

Half the morning is gone before I have fires laid under the smoking racks, with a stack of spare wood for that and for the regular cooking fire. It is going to be hard to get anything else done besides fetching wood. Then I have to haul water for the cooking pot, I mean basket, and by that time, I will have to haul firewood again. I sigh and pick up the water hauling basket. Fortunately, the stream is not far, but it is shallow and hard to dip from. I will have to remember to make a pool for dipping. Another project. Certainly not for today.

At last the cooking basket is full of water, and the rocks are hot enough to drop in; I can slowly raise the temperature of it, if I keep at it, maybe to boiling. Now, finally, for the meat itself. Trimming the fat away is pitifully easy. There's damned little fat on the poor animal. He was young and lean. I can spit and smoke a couple of roasts and some ribs for eating this week. And we can eat soup for awhile. But the rest of the meat will have to be cut into thin sheets, or strips, and attached somehow to the skeletal frames outside.

Somehow. I have been avoiding that problem because I have no idea how to deal with it. Well, one problem at a time. First, I will peel back the pelt as I cut so as not to expose the meat all at once to the bacteria in the air. Then, when I have the pelt free, I can peg that to the side of the longhouse, fur side in, and scrape it later when I have more time. I do not have the remotest idea of how to proceed with that chore. I read somewhere that squaws chew the skins to make them pliable. But certainly not with the fur still on them! Tanning! That was how you did it. With tannin which comes from some kind of bark. Maybe Johnny will know. Or maybe it is in one of his books. I hope the pelt will not stiffen up on me before I can figure out how to treat it.

I try cutting off thin layers of meat, but it refuses to come away in large pieces. I soon have a pile of small bits that are only good for the soup pot—basket. But as I work, I get better at it, and ultimately I have a pile of longer strips. These I take outside. I just look at the racks. The fires are ready for adding the green wood, and I am not prepared.

I carefully drape the hard-won strips of meat over the wooden skeleton and sit down to think. If I do not sit down I will cry. I smell something burning. It is my breakfast. I wolf it down, charcoal and all, and feel slightly better. A raven comes down from a nearby tree and inspects the remains of my breakfast. I give them to him, a little way from the fires so he will be more comfortable about eating, and resume my contemplation of the problematic racks.

Everything was so pleasant yesterday. So simple. All I had to do was follow Johnny's lead. No responsibility of my own. It all flowed. Is there any use asking Brother Elk to fillet himself and spit himself on these racks? No, of course not. The mood is gone, the exaltation entombed under years of drudgery. Women's work.

"Well, now what, Brother Raven? Do I just dump all the meat in the cooking pot and forget about smoking it? Do I admit that it's too much for me?"

Brother Raven caws disdainfully and flutters up to my pile of green alder sticks. He picks one up in his claws.

"Hey, put that down! I worked hard cutting those, dammit! And not so you could fly off with them!" I make a grab for him. He drops the stick and flies away, protesting loudly. He has dropped the stick so it lies crosswise over another. I stare at it. Some kind of lattice to weave the strips through? I try laying several of the longer sticks across the width of the framework. That looks like it could do something. That is what the forks in the sticks are good for, to hold other sticks. And the smaller sticks go between so I can weave the strips of meat through—no, the strips aren't big enough. I have seen these racks used on TV I think, but they were for smoking huge slices of salmon! If I'm going to use them for small strips of elk, I'll need lots more sticks in between. If I had enough, maybe I could weave the strips of meat through the green sticks and make a sort of mat! If it is firm enough, maybe I could turn it over to smoke dry the other side. It works, sort of. I feel so clumsy. My fingers just will not do what I know they should be able to do. Maybe with practice. After all, I have not taken a class in this sort of thing, and as for learning it at my mother's knee, my mother would have been horrified. She could never understand why anyone would want to camp out when they had a perfectly good bed to sleep in and a fine range to cook on at home.

"Thank you, Brother Raven, For the cooking lesson! I'm sorry I yelled at you. Come for scraps, anytime!"

It does not hurt to be polite, certainly not in this world, when you never know who or what you could be talking to. The raven could be Johnny's great grandmother.

I have made one rude mat which looks rather like a kindergarten effort (I can hear shy brown women giggling at my ineptness), when I remember my boiling basket. Sure enough, the water is cooling, and the fire has almost gone out.

I notice another discouraging fact; putting rocks in the water also fills the water with ash and grit. How can you make soup out of that? Grit soup. It is going to have to be strained into another basket, of course. They must have heated the water in one basket and poured the hot water over the meat in the other. That is for next time. For now this pot (basket) is going to be crunchy. Also bland. I have nothing else to put in it. I do not know any of the local edible plants, and I have no salt. The salt. Right.

At least there is a thin layer of fat congealing in the grit on the top of the water. I scoop it off and put that in a small cedar trough I found in the longhouse. I do not know what the trough is supposed to be for, but I am using it for soapmaking. More firewood. Especially green alder, because I have used all the sticks I cut to make the mat. I do not seem to be making any progress. I can not get ahead of the fires long enough to accomplish anything. I think I am forgetting something besides the salt. The lye. While I am picking up driftwood on the beach, I scoop a couple of wide, shallow depressions in clay that has fallen from the bank above, a minor slide area. I grimly check the remaining bank above camp. It seems stable enough. But one never knows. I fill the depressions I have made with sea water and hope the sun shines enough to do the rest.

The green alder is another problem. I have to go some distance for it. Although the alder thicket is not close, it is not far enough away that I will get lost. It has figured into the campsite location. For the first time

I wonder if Johnny is the only one to have used this spot for a camp. I imagine company, and welcome any inspiration they might offer while I hack down a pile of longer poles for the mats, and drag them back to camp. The green twigs I have to lop off will make great smoke.

The fires are built up again. Now to start the lye before going back to the butchering. I remember little about what I read. Seems to me the method used was "dripping." How do you drip water through wood ashes? Slowly, probably. I look around for a suitable container. I find an old basket with holes in it that Johnny has full of dry moss. I dump out most of the moss and scoop the basket full of cold, wood ashes, then set it over the trough of grease and pour water over the ashes. And then some more water. Until finally I am getting a little seepage through the bottom. Good.

Back to the elk. I have a nice pile of strips before I feel it is time to get more wood. On my way out to the alder grove I find the cooking smells have collected a hungry swarm of gulls, swooping down on my meat. I shoo them off. Screaming protest, they settle not far away and I know they will be back as soon as I am out of sight. I need a scarecrow—a scaregull. While searching for a container for the lye, I have noticed a small empty metal can in the house in a corner. It was a pop can that I assume Johnny found littering the beach somewhere. Maybe it washed up from a boat passing. I fetch it, fill it with small pebbles, and try the rascal. It makes a satisfactory racket. I chase the gulls down the beach, waving it madly as they depart for quieter beaches. They will probably be back, but meanwhile, I can get on with my wood gathering.

Back in the alder grove I notice a clump of familiar weeds. The leaves look like carrot tops. I pull one up, curiously. The root is long, thin and cream colored. I smell it. Smells like carrot. I break the root and touch the cut edge to my tongue. A little bitter perhaps, certainly not a garden carrot, but definitely familiar and not unpleasant tasting. It would do nicely for seasoning, but they certainly would not be filling; ten of them would not equal one supermarket carrot. I must find Johnny's book of plants and check it to be sure. I have heard that edible plants have poisonous look-a-likes.

There must be edible plants all around me, as well as poisonous ones. Plants that are good for seasoning, plants that make soap, plants that are good for headaches, rheumatism, boils, hemorrhaging, and indigestion. Plants that poison sharks, plants that color baskets, plants that make baskets for that matter, and not only baskets, but ropes, fishing line, nets, clothing, glue. The list must go on indefinitely. And I know none of them. Or next to none. There must have been a whole science of wild plants, using every part of the plant; all of it is lost.

The Indian woman had to know so much, invent constantly, and depend on an uncertain, random supply of raw materials for everything. It could take days, or weeks, to find the right herb for a sick child. And who minded the child while the mother was out hunting medicine? No wonder they lived in longhouses with several families. The old women collected the plants. Witch women. Or witch doctors. Medicine men. To free the rest for tending fires. Which reminds me. I have fires of my own to tend. If I could find plants and berries I could dry them to keep until the next season. God, another chore. It is endless. Why not collect enough berries and seeds, or whatever propagated the plants, and plant them close to the camp? It would save endless trouble for a permanent camp.

Once my fires are fed I try weaving another mat of meat strips. I am definitely getting more practiced, but I cannot make enough headway to inspire anything like confidence. Especially since the meat falls off when I build up the fire and has to be wiped off and put back.

When the meat I have already cut runs out, I go back inside to cut more. A pool of gray-brown water has collected in the trough of grease. It feels greasy, not soapy. I put water on it. Nothing. More lye? Still nothing. You must have to heat it. Damn. I throw a couple of fire rocks into the mixture and stir some more. Still no suds. I remove the cooled rocks from the grease and put them back into the fire to reheat. The greasy rocks smoke and sputter and flare. Probably good for starting fires in the morning, but too smoky a process for indoors. I wrestle the trough out the door and over to one of the smoking fires. A couple of real kettles to set over the fire sure would be nice. I put some fire rocks into the smoking fires, add more wood, and go back to cut more strips of meat.

Back to my butchering, with a definite lack of enthusiasm. The carcass looks bigger all the time. My arms begin to ache from stretching up to work with the knife, but the strips of meat begin to come away more easily and in longer pieces. It is tedious work but it uses different muscles than the picking up and carrying of wood. I am going to ache all over when this day is through. A third mat load of meat takes only half the time of the first one, which is still too much time, but I am encouraged. The soup water is simmering and smells pretty good. It looks awful though; I only hope I can strain it.

Hot rocks, into two baskets now, more firewood; damn I am getting low again. It is beginning to settle into a rhythm. A mindless repetition that is horribly familiar The fires need constant tending. If I do not feed them, their life will bleed away. More wood, more hot rocks, weave another mat, cut more strips, strip the carcass bare.

Then, unbelievably, the elk skin is free. I drape it, muscles straining painfully, over two of the roof poles outside. Tentatively, I run the back of the knife over the fatty tissue on the inside of the skin. Nothing happens. I try the sharp edge and make a tiny cut. That will not work. I am too tired to think of another method. I give up and go to turn another mat of meat to expose the other side. Several pieces of meat fall off. I put them back. They burn my fingers. The bubbling gray grease is not making soap. I must be doing something wrong. I am doing everything wrong!

I sit down heavily on a log and my hand rests on the knife blade. The sting is a blow to my already reeling nerves. I look down at the knife, blade upward upon the log, and at my hand with its thin red line of drops against the white skin of my palm. Angry tears ooze with the blood. The cut is monumentally unfair. How could I have done this? I am very careful with knives, especially with this one; it is a tool and weapon and more. And not to be replaced by running down to the discount hardware store. I don't treat it casually. I don't treat it carelessly. I know better than to risk cutting myself here where there is no doctor, no pharmacy, no medicine or bandages.

I could bleed to death before anyone came to help. I run to the water and plunge my hand into the coldness. It feels great. I take my hand out and examine it critically. It is not a serious cut. I wrap it tightly with a not too clean bandanna. It has stopped bleeding. If it becomes infected, Johnny will have to take me back to get it treated. For now, it hurts. It will hamper my already inadequate efforts at camp-keeping. And it has upset me beyond reason. Why did it happen? I do not believe in accidents. It feels like a deliberate assault.

I look around. The camp is impersonal, imperturbable, uninvolved, innocent. If anyone else is here, they are not hostile, only amused by my bungling. No. The agency that did this to me is not outside me. It is inside. I have done this to myself. But why? I take a deep breath and groan. My muscles all ache. There is my answer.

I am falling back into the same old pit of mindless physical labor I groveled in for so many years. The same well-remembered narcosis has already blotted out whole areas of perception. My muscles are screaming for relief. There is not enough oxygen for both brain and muscle. I can either think or move, not both. And the ache. Oh, God, the familiar ache, as bands of misery tighten around my skull. I thought I had finished with all this. I do not want to go back. Back to four babies, two of them in diapers at once. The mess, the eternal mess, always more than I could cope with, the crying, the fear, the awful responsibility, the dreary weight of four walls, imprisonment stretching onward forever. My youth spent, my health weakened. Trapped!!!

She will not go back to being a grub. She has found her wings! She is fighting for her life. For her freedom. She? . . . I! The newly winged me is rejecting this return to the grub she once was, and is using the knife to reprimand me. I resent the betrayal, but I understand it.

I am sitting, staring into the fire when Johnny's whistle startles me. The tide has come and gone out again. The day is over. I am an unholy mess; dirty, greasy, smoky. I have not bothered to comb my hair, the soup is not edible, and the venison will never be cured. I have not accomplished any of the things I had hoped to. I straighten my aching back and go painfully to meet my man.

TWELVE

J ohnny laughs when he sees me. It is not the most tactful thing he
could do.

"I'm not going to ask what you did today," he says. "I could smell
this place all the way down to the dig."

I gesture. I am too tired to do much else. Johnny surveys the
camp. I look at it through his eyes. Five smoking fires are going, four
of them with racks of meat, one with two roasts and ribs, and a heav-
enly smell is coming from the steaming basket inside the house. The
pelt is draped conspicuously over the side of the building. Johnny
whistles gratifyingly. I, too, am impressed. I seem to have accomplished more than I realized.

"I have one conspicuous failure, though," I admit. Johnny waits.
I point to the steaming trough. He walks over and looks into it. "It
stinks. What is it supposed to be?"

"It is supposed to be soap. It didn't work. I must be doing something wrong."

There is a long silence. Johnny is frowning. The air has changed
subtly. His approval has become qualified.

"How long have you been boiling it?" He asks carefully.

"Who knows? Maybe three hours? Maybe less."

"I think it takes a long time. Put more fire rocks in it and let's eat.
I'm starving."

Before we can eat I must strain the soup. I skim the top, then
Johnny helps me pour the rest through a loosely woven basket into

the other boiling basket. I fish out the meat trimmings from the bottom and rinse off the sludge. The bones go to the raven. The resulting broth is not terribly gritty and has only a slight charcoal taste. It is bland, but it tastes pretty good with the smoked meat.

I am too tired to enjoy the meal, but I need the nourishment. I get up after awhile to change the rocks in the soap trough. The gray mass is bubbling and seething like a lava porridge. It has thickened and become translucent.

I cannot hide my jubilation. I pull out the stirring stick and cautiously test the hot brew. It seems to have turned slippery.

"Hot damn. I did it!!" I am prouder of this than of everything else I have done all day, and relieved. At last I can get clean. Johnny continues to eat. I ignore him. With renewed energy I clean out the first soup basket and heat water in it, stripping impatiently as it heats and lathering myself in the lukewarm water. It feels unbelievably good to be clean!

I throw my filthy clothes into the basket of water with some of the soap to soak. I sit down beside Johnny, totally nude and utterly relaxed. "One of the true blessings of civilization is the luxury of being clean!" I am suddenly limp, as though the dirt and grease were all that was holding me upright.

Johnny gets up stiffly and walks away from the fire.

"Johnny? Don't you want to wash? It feels so good!"

He does not answer. I prattle on, blindly, hardly aware of what I am saying. "There must be a plant that makes suds. This way was too hard. I'll go through your books and see if I can find one. And some of the other plants we use all the time. I thought I'd collect their seeds or whatever and plant them near camp so we won't have to wander all over the woods looking for them. We could even grow our own cedar!!"

"While you're at it, why don't you just brew up a batch of asphalt and pave the whole beach; so much cleaner!! I'm sure if you put your Protestant overachieving mind to it, you could tidy up the whole fucking wilderness overnight!!"

His anger is a physical blow. His words cut like the knife blade into my unsuspecting flesh. I worked so hard. I tried. I am too tired to bear this . . . injustice. I cannot even protest; I can hardly believe the rebuke. Tears are streaming down my cheeks. I am sobbing uncontrollably. I run inside, wrap myself in a sleeping robe, and sob myself to sleep.

When I wake the next day, Johnny is on the other sleeping bench, asleep. It is late according to the position of the sun. I carry the racks of meat out into the air, painfully. My muscles protest yesterday's abuse. Johnny has put the racks into slots in the beams of the house, which look as though they were designed to hold them.

I start the cooking fire and put rocks in it and haul water for washing clothes. To hell with Johnny. I worked hard for it. I want to be clean. I deserve it, and I shall have it. I do not know what his problem is, but it is his, not mine. Whatever he objected to, I did with the best of intentions. I rejected his rule of doing things the old way with my soapmaking. How was I to know? What does he think I am, a mind reader? Yes. Exactly. He expects me to know what is in his head. And I never will.

I am dipping water from the stream when I notice the animal tracks. Bear. I have never seen a bear track before except in pictures, but it is huge and unmistakable. I look around quickly, but I am alone. The sun is shining reassuringly, the stream flows noisily, gushing cold water around my hands. My cut is sore but healing nicely. Not inflamed. I go about my water hauling as though I had not seen the tracks. That explains why Johnny is still here and asleep. He must have been up part of the night because of the bear. And I did not hear a thing. I have total trust in him in spite of last night's misunderstanding.

Now that I am aware of them, I see the tracks all around the camp. I had not noticed them before. An oversight I should not have made. All of my clothes are in the wash basket, soaking. What the hell. I pour in the rest of the water and start adding hot rocks. If the bear comes back, I will have wet clothes, but at least they will be clean. I dip in handfuls of the soft soap and stir it up well with my stirring stick. The cold water will have unset some of the protein stains, like the blood, and as the water heats it will loosen the dirt and grease. In spite of the primitive conditions, I just might get a clean wash. It is not a procedure you might hear advertised on TV, but it sounds efficient. There seem to be extra clothes in the basket. I fish out Johnny's shirt. He has put his clothes in with mine. A gesture of contrition. A mute apology. So like him. I snort, somewhat mollified.

I decide against re-lighting the smoking fires under the racks of elk meat. There is no use tempting fate. Johnny has said it is the smell of the smoking meat that attracts the animals. Sun drying does not smell as strong, and the meat is already partially smoked and drying nicely by itself. Maybe a few days in the sun will do it. The warm air is good for drying clothes also. Once I get them out they should dry fast.

I make another run to the stream for water for a rinsing basket. Everything is still quiet. The bear must be sleeping as heavily as Johnny is. I cut myself off a piece of the roasted ribs left from last night and eat it cold.

By the time Johnny gets up, I have all the bushes around the house draped with our clothing. He looks at the laundry without comment, and points instead to the tracks.

"I saw them." I answer. "I slept through our visitor."

Johnny goes to the door, which I have opened against the wall and pulls it shut so I can see the outside of it. I gasp. Deep gouges rake it from end to end, dents and splintered areas make it look as if a battering ram has hit it repeatedly. It is very distressed wood indeed. But it held.

"He must have made a racket to wake the dead! How could I have slept through that?!!"

"I thought you were dead. You didn't move. I actually checked once to see if you were breathing. She roared like kingdom come, charging that door. She prowled around here for hours. I thought she'd never leave. She was mad and damned determined. I figure she'll come back after she's had some sleep. We can't leave that meat out much longer. If she ever gets a taste of it, we'll never get rid of her."

"Black bear?"

Johnny shrugs. "Almost has to be. There aren't any grizzlies down this low. Prints are too small, too. But don't discount her. A female with cub is as deadly as a grizzly when she's riled."

"How do you know it's a female?"

He points around the camp to some small prints around the edge of camp I have not noticed. Will I ever learn?

Johnny stirs around the camp for awhile, hauling wood and water indoors, and then, impatient, scouts for short distances around the area. All seems quiet. The stewed jeans are pretty clean considering, and drying faster than I hoped, even if they are a bit stiff. I remember my salt hole and check it cautiously. It has not changed at all. It will take a long time. Johnny comes up behind me and together we stare at the puddle. "Too many contaminates in the residue," he observes. His tone is scratchy from nerves and lack of sleep, not disapproval of the project. I do not comment.

I put on my clean, stiff, only slightly damp clothes. Things are far too quiet. Johnny is restless. He washes, again without a word, puts on clean clothes, and determines to go to work.

"I'll tell them I'm taking a couple of days off. We'll go for a canoe trip until that she-bear gets tired of the meat scent." He wants to put the meat racks back inside, but I will not let him. "I worked hard on that meat and it isn't ready. It will spoil if it isn't dried enough. I'll stay here and defend it."

Johnny makes a rude noise. He leaves the knife in plain sight on the bench log and disappears.

It is a relief not to have him pacing nervously around the campsite. I shoo away a couple of stray gulls who hover over my racks, but I do not use the cans. I do not want to wake up the bear if she is sleeping in the vicinity. Johnny does not seem to think she has gone far. He has left a shell scraper for working on the elk skin, so I set about that chore, discarding the fatty membranes. They are already beginning to smell. I give them to the gulls. I hope they will give me notice if the bear should come; they screech and fight so much all the time that I will notice if they become quiet.

I am still smarting over Johnny's insensitivity. He brings me here and dumps me into a totally alien environment and then expects me to work miracles. Not only do I have to survive but I have to operate according to some obscure code of rules that I doubt even *he* understands. All right, I did know that Johnny's ancestors never made soap like mine did. I cheated. But they could have done it. They had all the ingredients! If I could do it under these circumstances, they could have. And all right, I knew how. That is, I knew *that it was done* and had read how it was done, enough to guess at the procedure, and in fact to do it. They had no such foreknowledge. So am I supposed to stay as dirty and greasy as they must have been? I know, I already said dirt is in the eye of the beholder. And, its moral significance belongs to an alien culture. It was irrelevant to them, and it is irrelevant to Johnny. Although he must have a problem when he goes back to town. I know he cheats. He has to. He is too clean: When in Rome ... And that applies to me, too. When I am here I play by these rules, or leave.

The afternoon sun begins to warm things up. I soak it up, my tired muscles bask in it, relaxing me. The monotony of the task I am performing is soothing. I almost drowse. Then, unaccountably, I am nervous. I look up and around every other minute, and find myself getting up and pacing as Johnny was doing. I decide to take myself seriously. I move the skin indoors, and begin to take in the drying racks, carefully, one at a time. I have two inside already, and am carrying the third, when I see him. A cougar.

He is standing by the stream, watching me, not twenty feet away. I keep moving slowly, carrying the rack, watching the cat out of the corner of my eye, and keeping the rack roughly between us, so I can use it as a shield if he should charge. His appearance is a total shock. I have trouble comprehending what is happening. I was expecting a bear. A cougar is not in the program. I wonder what would happen if the bear should show up. They might scare each other off. Or maybe there was no bear. No. The bear was real enough. Those were not cougar tracks. And Johnny would not make that mistake.

I slowly maneuver myself inside the door, drop the rack, and grab for the door. For a moment I am exposed, defenseless in the doorway facing him. The cat has not moved. He is watching me, waiting.

My hands are shaking as I lower the heavy log barricade over the inside of the door. I am panicked. At the same time I am torn. Johnny is out there. I am barricading him out. He is due back anytime, and his knife is still out there on the log where he left it. He is weaponless, and I cannot even warn him. The walls will muffle my voice.

But I have no choice. My hands and arms lower the log without directives from my head. It is counter weighted so it is easy to maneuver. It can be removed quickly, also, but it might not be quickly enough. Johnny would want me to barricade the door. He would order me to do it. But it hurts me to do it, just the same.

I wonder if I would be able to hear Johnny's whistle from inside. If he whistles, the cougar would hear it and be alerted. And Johnny would be unaware. If I hear Johnny coming I can unbarricade and even open the door, because he would have the cat's attention. Then I could yell to warn him and between us, maybe we could scare the cat off long enough for him to get inside.

Is this part of why Johnny was so nervous? Then it is his own fault for leaving me alone. Damn him. I am crying. The cat will soon be occupied with the remaining rack of meat. I resent that. I begrudge him that meat. I worked hard for it. I killed for it. And the cat bully comes along, flexes his muscles, and takes it away from me.

Surely Johnny will be concerned and aware. If I could feel the presence of the cougar surely he will sense it. He would not alert the animal, who is preoccupied no doubt with eating my meat, and he would see that I am safely locked inside. He could turn around and go back to the dig. He could bring back help. Surely someone there has a weapon, a gun. If it is this wild around here, they should at least be prepared.

It is not a big cat after all. Not much larger than a Great Dane. Not like the tiger of my recurring nightmare. And this time I am alone. The children are gone. Safe. It is just me and the cat outside and Johnny, somewhere, on his way home. It is not so much to worry about. But I am worried. I am scared. Irrationally scared. My teeth rattle in my head and I am drenched in cold sweat. Damn it. I am safe enough inside. I put another piece of wood on my fire, and pick up the abandoned rack of meat. I wrestle it into its place in the corner, cursing my clumsiness. Finally I wrap myself in a sleeping skin and sit down by the fire.

This is not the same as in my nightmare. But it is too close. And suddenly it feels even closer. The cat is inexplicably on the roof. This is not what I expected. A cat stalking me was in my nightmare. But this one should be busy with my rack of meat. After all, that is what he came for. Isn't it? Why is he torturing me? He scrabbles heavily around on the roof, and a few boards move and creak ominously. Something large clatters down and falls to the ground outside. I can see no hole in the roof. What if the roof is not fastened down tightly? Damn Johnny. I know he did not use nails at all. The house is flimsily built, just like the rude shelters of his ancestors. It is not designed to withstand the attacks of a large animal, although it took the charge of the bear last night.

What did they do? Surely they had problems with wild animals. They had dried meat and fish and they smoked it. And there were more animals then. But the answer is obvious. There were whole families of them living in these houses. And dogs outside. Lots of hunters around to kill the beasts. And I am alone. If the cougar comes through the roof I am helpless. I have barricaded him out and myself in. I could only distract him with meat and try to escape. There are no weapons inside except for a whale harpoon that Johnny made, leaning against the far wall. It has a long pole, but it is fragile, meant only for carrying the detachable point, not for use as a spear. It would splinter if any pressure were put on it. It is worse than useless because the point would only infuriate the cat, not kill him.

I need a nice gun, that is what I need. And Johnny does not believe in guns. At least when my ancestors came to this country they built cabins of heavy logs and armed themselves with firearms. Fire. Animals are supposed to be afraid of fire. I have one. I put another log on it. What else are they afraid of? Noise. Of course. The gulls stayed away from the meat racks when I rattled a canful of rocks. Where is that? Outside by the last rack, dammit. What is there inside that I can use to make noise? I could scare the cougar and warn Johnny at the same time. Something metal. There is nothing metal in this place! Something else Johnny does not believe in. A gas can! Johnny has a spare for the motor bike!! It is hidden in the corner

under some old ropes. If I can find something to bang on it with. . . .
A fire rock will do. I grab one and start denting the empty gas can
with all my strength. It does make a fine din. The scrabbling on the
roof ceases abruptly while the cat considers. I bang away, howling as
well, adding my yells to the drumming. That does it. There are sounds
of the cat leaving the roof. I can barely hear it over my own noise, but
I do. I keep up the drumming long after my arms are tired and my
voice has become hoarse.

"Ruth? You all right? Open up!!"

It is Johnny's voice outside. I race for the door and frantically
push at the log. It comes free much too slowly. Johnny grabs me and
holds me. I am hysterical.

"The cat? Where's the cat?" I sob, reaching to pull the door shut
behind him. "Is he gone?"

"You scared the shit out of every animal for miles," Johnny is
laughing. "What cat? There's not even a gull out there. I figured the
bear came back to give you an excuse for a concert."

"It was a cougar. You mean he's really gone? He didn't even stop
for the meat?"

"You sounded like all the fiends of hell let loose in here. No dinner's worth that kind of torture. He wasn't a rock-and-roll fan."

It is hard to tell whether I am laughing or crying. Sometimes they
are the same. "At least I got my laundry done," I blubber.

THIRTEEN

"Laundry? Damn it woman! Will you cease your bloody Christian preoccupation with eradicating dirt!!"

"I'm sorry! Really. I had no idea it was so imprinted. I know lots of women who are much worse. I'll try. But I can't erase three thousand years quite that fast. Let me taper off? A bath a week? Just until I get acclimatized. Cold turkey is rough at my age."

"All right. I shouldn't let a little thing like that bug me. But you were doing so well and then you reverted. You would pick the very things that symbolize the whole world we're supposed to be leaving behind."

Johnny goes out and returns with the remaining rack of meat. The cougar apparently has not touched it.

"Perhaps he prefers fish. Some cats do," I offer.

Johnny is not smiling. "Ruth," he says, "There are no prints out here. Not one cat paw print anywhere. Plenty of bear, but no cat. And no tracks or scratches on the roof."

"But he was on the roof. I heard him distinctly. He knocked something heavy off. I was afraid he would tear off some shingles and come inside. He must have left some marks!"

"Come look for yourself."

Johnny is right. I can find no trace of my visitor.

"I didn't just imagine him. He was real!!"

"I'm not doubting you. Come show me where he was standing when you first saw him."

The mud by the stream where the cat had stood watching me is undisturbed. An animal as heavy as that cougar would have left an imprint in the soft mud. We search up and down the stream bed within sight of the house. There is nothing.

"First, I make a hoof print as an imaginary elk that I shouldn't have made, and now a real cougar doesn't make one he should have made. What is going on here?'

"It's good that you should connect the two. I think there is a relationship."

"How?"

"Both are signs to you: the first that you must believe, that the imaginary can become real, and the second, well perhaps the same? If the prints had been there you would think nothing unusual."

"Now wait a minute. I know that cougar was not imaginary. I was expecting a bear. I was so surprised when the cat showed up. If I had been going to make up a beast out of nervous overexcitement or something, I would have made up a bear."

"Maybe."

"Definitely. It was a real cougar. The roof! Something heavy rolled off the roof. Let's go look. That has to be there."

It is. On the far corner, just around the corner out of sight, where it could easily have rolled, is a human skull. A naked, white, toothless head grinning at me. I cannot speak.

Johnny whistles softly.

"Your cat was definitely not an ordinary cat. Are you sure the cat doesn't have some special meaning for you?"

"Yes. The dream. When he appeared I thought of the dream about the tiger right away. I have a recurrent nightmare about a tiger. But this was different! In my dream the cat is a huge tiger. I can see his stripes and that enormous head and those paws; and the colors, orange and black, unmistakable, and the distinctive noise he makes. This was a mangy beast by comparison, beige and only a fraction of the size. He snarled and scrabbled and screamed, cougar noise. Not the same at all."

"Reality is always paler and smaller than the dream."

"What do you mean by that? Are you telling me that my nightmares are coming to life?"

"Possibly. Why not?"

"Jeezus. Because they don't. They can't. If that were true, then it wasn't the meat the cougar was after at all. It was me? But the kids! They weren't with me. In the dream it was always the children the tiger ate. Not me."

"Children in the plural? Or just one?"

"One at a time. I don't know. I don't remember. Perhaps only one. What difference? . . ."

"Beats me. It's your dream. I'm just trying to help. Don't yell."

"But it's so crazy. Was he after me? As a child? My God, you could be right. Or the child that is in me, is part of me, and always will be. The one that got shoved aside, ignored in favor of my other children. Johnny, do you think so?"

"Does it seem right to you? It's your dream, your subconscious— your cat."

"It does. I guess. It could be. But why? Why should my old outworn nightmare be coming to life here? In this place? And the skull?'

Johnny grins. "It's been obvious from the first; the spirits are trying to communicate with you."

"But why me? I'm not particularly sensitive, at least not that kind of 'sensitive'; these must be your spirits, here in this place, your ancestors. Aren't they? Why should they speak to me? Why not to you?"

"Spirits are spirits. There are many spirits, some whose names we know. They don't belong to anyone. They belong in another dimension. Some linger in certain places on earth. Anyone who is particularly sensitized, tuned in to the right frequency to intercept them, as you seem to be here and now, is going to receive some kind of impression. The kind of impression you get is not something you can choose. Mediums get vibrations from all kinds of places, not just from their own ancestors."

"I don't like it. This is scaring me. What do they want of me? And what is next? The bear? Was that meant for me, too?"

Johnny laughs. "I don't think so. You were totally unconscious through the whole thing. Maybe the bear was meant for me. To punish me for yelling at you."

"Do you think so? That's delightful! She didn't come back after you put your clothes into the soapy water to apologize! But she left lots of prints."

"I don't need as much convincing as you do!!"

"Are you teasing me? I don't know what to believe in this crazy place."

"Let's have some dinner and forget the whole thing. We can take a little trip first thing tomorrow and come back when things have quieted down some. Though, it's my opinion that after your rock concert, there won't be an animal in the Northwest that would come near this camp if it were starving."

"You had to have been there," I say. "I don't relish the thought of spending the night here, though."

"You take your fears with you," Johnny observes. "Now which will it be, fish or elk for dinner?"

"Fish," I say with a noticeable lack of enthusiasm.

"Good. We'll go fishing. Beautiful evening for it. Do you good. Too much standing over smoking fires makes you crazy."

I do not argue. We launch the smaller canoe into a sea of antique green bottle glass. This boat trip, like everything else in my new life, is different from every other previous experience. The motion of our canoe is lulling, but never monotonous. The Pacific is still. There is almost no wind and Johnny's strength sends the long, silent canoe streaking through the water. It rides the waves effortlessly, the tiny flare at the top splitting the water and spitting it out cleanly on both sides, leaving the interior dry. I marvel out loud at the design.

"It's a small version of a Chinook. Hand carved of cedar. And a damned lot of work to make! The design is much like the Viking ships," Johnny says, pleased. "Those were used for war, too, as well as for long journeys. The Chinook is very maneuverable. It had to be to hunt whales and sea lions. In the hands of a skilled crew it could turn handsprings around a motorboat. Unless, of course, the motorboat had a Native American crew.

"This one is special. I did it the old way. I made myself worthy of the right to create a Chinook. It's a complicated ritual."

"Like earning the right to become an elk?"

"Very similar."

I lie back, enchanted by our motion. We skim the calm sea like a strange sea monster, flapping over the waves, startling an occasional stray gull. Except for our modern clothing we could be in any epoch in the last two thousand years. Impulsively, I pull off my clothes and hide them under the gear.

Johnny grins when he sees what I am doing. "You're the wrong color," he points out.

"I will be red in no time," I promise.

We are still within sight of shore, traveling parallel to it, headed north. There is no sign of habitation. No ships, no boats, no houses, no people. Just us in our beautiful canoe and the birds, in the whole of creation.

The sky has swelled to fill the empty horizon. It is a uniform blue with a couple of painted puffs of white for accent. Not even a jet trail marks its purity. Johnny pauses in his paddling to strip also. Then it really gets strange. I can feel the excitement of the day ease out of my body. It is not a deflation, but more of a relaxation of muscles that were tensed for action. My whole being has been tight and now it is resting. Peace overwhelms me.

I turn to look at Johnny. He is enjoying his work, and does not seem self-conscious about my interest. He is good at what he is doing and comfortable with his body. He even preens a bit for my benefit, deliberately baptizing me with a shower of drops from the paddle. It is a pleasant change to watch him from a front view. A week ago I would never have noticed him in a crowd. In Western clothing he tends to blend into invisibility. Naked, he glows. The late sun is picking up the bronze tints in his brown skin. The planes of his face and body are my bronze fortress against which the arrows of the outside world glance off harmlessly. I feel totally safe and loved. I revel in our closeness, all the more so because it is such a rare moment, perhaps never to be repeated. It must be made to last, for the lifetime of the sunset.

Johnny interrupts my reverie with the practical concerns of his dinner. He stops paddling and begins to fish. He throws me a line and I try my hand also. It does not seem to be unduly strenuous work. There are a couple of false alarms and the necessity for re-baiting my hook, but mostly I sit idly, riding the swell of the ocean's breast, totally comfortable. Then luck strikes. Johnny hauls in a smallish salmon and a few minutes later I am nearly pulled out of the canoe by my first big fish. Johnny comes to help and together we land a huge flapping sole, a strange looking creature with eyes in the wrong place. But they are tasty.

Johnny puts away the gear. "More fish than we can eat already," he says. "Want to smoke some of this?" He asks with a straight face. I groan. It is too pretty here to even think of work. And much too pretty to leave. We let the sole go, watching it sink slowly out of sight. Johnny moves slowly, in the general direction of camp, mostly letting the current carry us.

I have never sat through an entire sunset. I always grow impatient and busy myself with something else. Tonight I cannot think about anything else. My mind is in neutral. The only impressions I am receiving are of love, of beauty, of peace, the cooling wind on my sun-baked body, our gentle motion through the water, the flight of the gulls. I am at rest.

As we watch, the sky begins to darken subtly toward the east. The scene's houselights dim and a spotlight focuses on the death of the sun. It is a breathtaking performance. When the final curtain of darkness, lit with stars, stirs me, I awake.

I have not slept. I have been in some other state. The state of contentment surely, of suspended reality. Perhaps it is close to the nirvana of the Buddhists. The self righteous heaven of the Christians could not compare with it. I feel no consciousness of myself, only a blending of the consciousness I share with the air, and wind, and the infinite play of color in the light. I was not just a spectator, I too was a cloud suffused with the trembling light; first rose, them shading from copper to pink, now purple lined with purest gold. The fading drama leaves me empty, chilled. We return to camp, and in the lingering light, clean and cook our fish. We are quiet and drained, naked in the firelight. Finally, Johnny reaches for my hand and leads me inside. His lovemaking is soothing, an affirmation of our closeness. I curl myself into the curve of his body and know nothing more.

The tunneled edges of my dream are shaded. The light focuses upon a hallway. An impossibly large and long hallway. Where have I known such a place? Mumbled voices, coming at intervals down the corridor from transoms above regularly spaced doors, suddenly place me. A school. I am in a school hallway. I am small, and that is why it looks so large. I feel the uncomfortable squirm of self-deprecation beginning inside. Imminent humiliation fills the air like the sour smell of overheated children's bodies and chalk dust; it is fetid, nauseating. I am in the schoolroom. The chanting voices will cease and all attention will focus upon me. It will be my turn. There is nowhere to go, no safe place to hide. Only the long hallway lined with doors, and behind each door lies misery. They wait behind those doors. Sooner or later I will open one. Or if I wait too long, the bell will ring, and the doors will all open simultaneously and the suffering will engulf me.

I run down the corridor, regretting the telltale noise of my feet echoing in the empty hall. I hope for a stairway. There is always a stairway.

I am no longer in the school. There is no corridor, only dusty corners, but there is a stairway. It leads down a short flight of six wooden steps. And at the end of the steps is a door. A door with no handle. I am in the attic of an old house, the house of a friend who lives up the block. I am five years old. My friend is six. I cannot reach the stairs and the doorway; they lie beyond a field of open beams, past clouds of insulation and exposed wiring. I have been warned not to go there. It is not safe. I could be electrocuted.

The doorway leads to a room in the attic that no one ever enters. There is a window on the outside of the house for that room. But no one has been there. For years? Forever. There is something terrifying about a window from which no one ever looks. Especially to a child. Years later I will read about that room. The house used to be part of the underground railway, a hiding place for slaves before the Civil War. I know that in the dream, even though I am only five. It is part of my information bank about that room, but it does not help. It does not begin to cut into the fear.

I am fascinated by that room. And terrified of it. I *have* to go down those steps and open that door. I have tried before. My friend and I once made it part way down those stairs. The third step from the bottom. I remember so clearly. My friend stepped on it first. There was a spring. The door at the foot of the stairs began to open slowly. We fled in panic and never again tried to discover what was behind the door.

But now the door is the only way out. I have to open it if I want to escape. Otherwise I am trapped in the attic of my childhood forever. I cry; I plead. It is no use. The door must be opened. Slowly, carefully, blinded by my own tears, conscious of my childish whimpering, shaking and unreasonably afraid, I go, across the minefield of open beams. Certain of momentary death by electrocution, I creep to the stairs. Once they are reached, the panic mounts. Each step down feels like a movement closer to the grave. I steel myself and put my foot on the crucial third step. Slowly the door begins to creak open. I stand alone this time, paralyzed on that step and watch the door open.

I am no longer five. I am forty. And there is something in the doorway, or someone. A figure, full length, sways into view. Suspended by chains, a woman hangs. She is wrapped completely in a tattered, mended cloth. The material is stretched tightly over the outlines of her face. Her eyes stare, her mouth is open in a silent scream. Her hands are claws, clutching at the shroud. How long has she been there? The answer is clear. Since I was five. I begin to scream.

I scream and scream and I cannot hear a sound. My scream is as silent as hers. My scream *is* hers. I have never known such terror.

"Ruth! Ruth baby, please?!! It's okay now!!"

Johnny's voice penetrates my fear. I am screaming out loud. I can hear myself, but I cannot get through, get away, and I cannot stop screaming. I am totally panicked, hysterical. I keep clawing at him and at my face, trying to free my mouth of the obstruction.

FOURTEEN

Waking is like coming out from under an anesthetic. It takes a long time. Reality feels hollow and unreliable. Johnny makes me get up and follow him outside. I sit before the fire wrapped in the sleeping skin. The sun has warmth but it cannot penetrate my chill. Johnny gives me a cup of pine-needle tea, bitter and hot. My hands shake around the wooden cup.

I feel as though I have been ill. I am listless, and at the same time restless, irritable, and supersensitive. Johnny is watching me, concerned. Crossly, I refuse to speak. Make him ask. Finally, his curiosity wins.

"That was a helluva nightmare."

"Yes."

"Was it a new one, or had you had it before?"

"I never saw it before. That's not exactly true. I never dreamed it before. The *door* I have definitely *seen* before."

He is listening. I tell him the dream, hoping that the daylight telling might take away some of the terror. It does. But only some. "I do not want to dream that again, ever."

"Change of scenery. We'll take our little scenic trip. That should distract you."

"You take your fears with you, you said."

Johnny grimaces. "You've lived a long time without ever dreaming that dream."

"That's what scares me. Why now? I had buried that attic and those stairs and that door at the bottom. I haven't thought about it in years. It scared the shit out of me when I was small."

"It's still scaring you," Johnny points out.

"It is, yes. I wish I had gone on. Gone down those stairs when I was small and gone into that room. Then I would know. All the fear would be gone out of that memory. I'm sure the room was empty. I was sure of it even then. But now I'll never know. It can continue to scare me."

"You're afraid to open that door. Why? What do you think you'll find?"

"Something dead."

"Then you needn't fear it."

"No, not something dead. That's not it."

Johnny waits politely.

"Evil. Something horrible. Something I can't accept. In me."

He smiles, and says nothing.

"If someone, something, is trying to communicate with me, why can't it come out and say what it intends to? Why this piece-by-piece, clue-by-clue torment? First the cat, then the skull, and now this. It's not nice. It has my attention. What more does it want? I'm listening! I'm listening!"

"It is hard to reach the other side of consciousness. It has to be done through images, memories. It's a game of charades. And you have to guess."

"All right, the category is fear. But which one? There are so many. I've been afraid all my life. As a child I was afraid of every-thing. I was overprotected to the point of being smothered."

Johnny's grin has something of a sneer to it.

"I guess that's hard for you to understand," I continue. "Growing up on the reservation can't have been very sheltered."

"The only thing I was protected from was overprotection. And I suppose the 'better things of life.'"

"I didn't ask to be overprotected. It wasn't pleasant. And we weren't rich. I grew up civil-servant poor. Which means we had food on the table and the rent paid and no money left for anything else. It was a flat life with no beauty in it. Except for the books. If it hadn't been for the public library, I don't know what I'd have done. I thrived on the books. I sure didn't thrive on love. Some love was there.

I know it was there, but it was so hidden, so choked with bitterness and resentment that it was stunted. I grew up in spite of it."

Johnny is watching me sideways, as he pokes the fire.

"But you're a warm and loving woman," he observes.

I am touched. He can always seem to touch me this way. It must be the novelty. In my experience men do not say things like that. They will not give you the satisfaction. Maybe they think it gives you a hold on them, a weapon perhaps, to know what they really feel. This man is comfortable enough to let me inside his own skin. I cling to him and cry. For both of us. For all of the years of doing without the comfort of love.

When I can speak, I answer him. "And you, too. You're open and loving. More than any man I have ever known. How come?"

"Beats me. My aunt raised me. She was very proud of me. Wanted me to grow up to be a non-Indian, to 'amount to something.' I disappointed her when I came back here."

"Well, you please me. Very much. I love you."

"I know. It's a damned inconvenience. It isn't going to fit into either of our plans." He is patting my back, trying to tease me into control.

"You're my plan," I mutter. "The only one I seem to have."

He laughs. "That's a terrible responsibility. Except I don't believe you. I think you're just upset this morning; you had a bad night. You'll get over it."

"Do you really think that?"

"I'd like to. It could save us both a lot of grief. This has been a big vacation for you. One day you're going to go back. I live here."

"I have nothing to go back to. You're everything I have. We're stuck with each other. You have to admit, it's had its moments."

"Yes." He chuckles. "For you, too. I notice you've quit worrying about how old you are."

"You're right! I think it began when the Spirit World began to intrude on reality. My age and experience became an advantage instead of a handicap. I'm not who I used to be. The rules have all changed. That just adds to the nightmare."

He does not answer. He puts out the fire and begins to pack up. I wander off, dissatisfied.

I need Johnny to be loving and reassuring. Instead, he is honest. I do not want to hear that it might end. I am not ready for that possibility. The thought upsets me unreasonably.

The water is hidden by an ominous fog. I still am not warm. The vagrant sun gives me no security. The wind, which was benevolent last night, is a curse this morning. Its icy whips chase me down to the tide-swept sand where gulls squabble over a tidbit. The water seems dark and unfriendly for the first time. Waves crash with malevolence. I feel alien. What am I doing here? I need the comfort of the familiar; I need shelter, even luxury. A warm bed, a hot bath, hot food. Served to me, elegantly. Croissants with butter, café au lait on a sun drenched terrace; figs and cream and conversation. All the luxuries I always dreamed of, and even experienced on occasion. Will I ever know them again?

This is Johnny's world, not mine. He has chosen it. And I chose him. Could I go back? I do not want to go back to Richard. To the life I have been locked into for twenty two years. I want the luxuries, but I do not want what goes with them. I want it all; Johnny and the amenities. But he will not allow the amenities. He has had the chance. I know he has. He rejected it. And if I want him I will have to take him as I find him, along with the stark beach and the willful sun and the hostile sea.

Winters in town, maybe? Surely he does not have to spend all year here. It would be unpleasant here in the winter. We could both work. As long as we are together. I have to dream about impossible compromises. I cannot face the thought of life without him.

At the tide's edge the birds are still quarrelling. Their noise grows more insistent. A wave retreats from a flash of white, exposing an intriguing outline. I start towards it, glad of a diversion. The water covers the object again, playing games with it, unsettling the gulls. A scattering of ravens has joined the melee. I do not see the object until I am upon it.

The waves retreat momentarily, exposing the object for my eyes, as the gulls, finally conscious of my presence among them, rise to reveal a skull; a white, bleached, pitted, weathered human skull lying in the sand. Another one. I am hypnotized. Cold chills, not wind-borne, chase themselves down my spine. The water covers the skull again mercifully, entwining it with fronds of seaweed. The gulls are after a fish head lying beside it, not the skull itself. It has been some time since that skull held nourishment for any living thing.

I run back to get Johnny. I do not have to explain. He comes quickly. Salvage of the sea's discards has always been his tribe's pre-rogative. He takes one look, and pulls me away. We hurry to the canoe. He has packed it. We get in and push off. Johnny is in a hurry. I do not argue. We do not speak until we are well away.

"Johnny? Where are they coming from?"

"From a place that doesn't exist, as far as the U.S. government is concerned, anyway. It's an island that's not on any map or chart, that can't be found unless there is a specific need for it. It's my tribe's tra-ditional burial ground, and the later residents were all technically 'lost at sea.' We're supposed to bury our dead, in 'sanitary' cemeteries. That storm we had the other night must have stirred things up. There's another storm coming. Unseasonable. The spirits are restless. Their sleeping place is disturbed. All hell could break loose this time."

"Another storm coming? When?"

"Tonight, or tomorrow early. I want you to see the caves first before the waves get too high. I was going to camp, but maybe we should spend the night at the res. I ought to warn them about the skulls."

I am still as Johnny drives the canoe through obstinate fog. Rocks on both sides of us loom through their shrouds. Johnny ignores them like familiars. Every stroke of his paddle diminishes what is left of my sense of the real. I am sinking back into the gray wool of the nightmare. The only sound is the dripping of the paddle, the booming of the waves on an invisible shore to our right, and the crashing of waves around us as we pass through the pillars of lava. The fog splits up the sound and muffles it around us until it is useless to me as a guidepost. A canoe trip through a haunted landscape. A Disneyland tour of Never-Never Land, or more precisely, Never-More Land, quoth the raven. My ravens have squabbled over a skull. Very appropriate.

A towering obelisk brushes past us on the left. Johnny draws my attention to it. "The rock of the foolhardy warrior," Johnny announces and begins a story

Before our capture by the white men, the young men of our tribe climbed this rock to hunt for birds' eggs, and to test their climbing agility and courage. One day a young warrior spotted a ledge high on the side of the sheer rock face. He could see birds flying to and from the ledge, so he was sure there were nests on it, but no one with good sense would attempt to scale that slippery surface. But he was stubborn and had little experience, and he was determined to dazzle his companions with his nerve. He surveyed the cliff face closely and discovered, here and there, patches of moss among the coating of bird slime. There must be cracks or extrusions that allowed enough earth to collect to support the moss, and possibly to provide a hold for his clinging feet and hands. Sure enough as he gathered his nerve and began to test it, there were enough solid supports to allow him to progress up the wall. He, carefully, did not look down at the deep plunge to the sea below, and he didn't think about the trip back. He concentrated all his strength and energy and skill on the climb, and, with an almost superhuman effort, managed to attain the ledge. As he made the last heave to the ledge, he felt the foothold behind him give way. When he looked back, a large section of the cliff, including the near-est of the footholds he had used, had fallen away into the sea, far below. He gave a yell of relief and triumph, but it was not necessary to attract his comrades' attention. They had heard the rock fall and the splash below, and had come to see what caused it. They stared in amazement at their friend high on his ledge, almost out of reach of their voices.

They called to him to come down, pointing out that the tide was coming in and they were going to have to leave. The young man strutted for awhile, and stuffed his collecting

pouch with birds' eggs, and then, finally, when he could post-
pone it no longer, he went to the edge and looked down. The
drop into the sea was breathtaking, and he could see rocks
just under the surface and breaking through the surface all
around the base of the pillar. There was no clear spot to
dive into, should he be tempted. He took a deep breath and
looked back down the rock face the way he had come. The
damage from the falling rock was greater than he had anticipated. The only handholds left were twenty to thirty times
his length below him. Even if he could string together all his
gear and hang from them, he could not reach that far. He
would only hang there until he fell. There was no way back.

Johnny's voice falters and he is still.
"Go on, go on," I insist. "Then what did he do?"
Johnny continues slowly, as if picking his own way through
the story.

The young man looked down at his friends waving and
yelling far below him. They seemed such an impossibly long
way away. They were more precious to him than he had
thought. He longed to be among them, to laugh and joke
about his feat as they went back to the village. To their home.
He could almost see the shell-cluttered beach, the canoes
drawn up beside the long, handsome wooden buildings
fronted by their impressive crest poles, with the eagle, the
raven, and the grizzly grinning out over the water. The
smoking supper fires, good smells of food cooking, the chat-
ter and laughter of the women, the crying of a baby, and
exclamations over his catch of birds' eggs, all were so impossibly far away now.

He looked up. The cliff face above him was not as sheer
as the one below. There were other ledges, other footholds.
Perhaps if he kept climbing he might find another way down
on the far side of the rock. He had no choice. He climbed

and he climbed, desperately now. The voices of his comrades faded and disappeared. He dared not look to see if they had gone. It was his life at stake now. Up and up he climbed, higher and higher into the clouds. And finally he was on top. He sank down exhausted and it was some time before he could gather courage enough to look down the other sides of the rock pillar. He could see the whole world from his perch but it did him little good, because he could not fly. He crawled first to this edge and then to the next. The wall he had just climbed was the only one that could be climbed. The far sides hung out over the rest of the pillar supports, how far he could not guess, and there was nothing he could hold onto to get back under them. He was neither fly nor spider.

Johnny's voice dies away.

"Well, what happened? Did he get down?" I demand.

"No. I suppose if you were foolhardy and lucky enough to climb that rock, you might find an odd bone fragment, or a piece of his collecting pouch there, if the birds and the storms had not disposed of them all years ago."

"That's terrible. Johnny? Is that the way the story is always told, or are you just a champion storyteller? I could almost see the boy, a doll-sized figure standing up there in the clouds."

"I just got into the tale this time. I never heard it or told it like that before. It was almost as if I were climbing that rock myself." He looks at me and grins.

"I'm glad I'm down here. With you. Instead of food for the eagles."

"Me, too." He is disturbed by the story, identifying with the isolation of it, I guess. And he has shared that with me.

He has shared his skin with me when I needed comfort; I would like to give him mine. But mine is too small, and the wrong color, and I suspect it would not give him much comfort anyway. It's not helping me much right now.

FIFTEEN

J ohnny is silent, his end of the canoe weighty with his thoughts.
I do not intrude, watching the ominous parade of rocks through
the fog and wondering how many ships lay at the bottom of the sea
because of them. What monstrous volcanic firestorm spilled these
huge raw chunks into the sea? And what of the people who had lived
in the shadow of the Olympic range while it was going on? Where
could one hide when the sky was falling?

I put the question to Johnny. He shrugs. "There are tales about
the feuds between mountain gods. They would grow angry with one
another and throw fire rocks," he says. His tone is distant, as is his
interest. Back on the pillar with that luckless boy, no doubt.

So someone was around to witness at least part of the volcanic
activity. Poor terrified souls. Where do you run when the gods are
displeased? And there was the mud slide back at the dig. The whole
hillside covered the village. That must have happened more than once
on these unstable banks. And there were waves, larger than those
caused by monster storms, though there were those also. There must
have been tidal waves. All cultures have a Big Wave legend, especially these tribes along the coast. I remember reading that somewhere. In my other life.

Gradually, I become conscious of the increasing noise level. It is
like a roar from a waterfall somewhere ahead in the deceptive fog. I
look anxiously at Johnny, consumed by my thoughts of disasters. He
points ahead with the paddle.

"The caves. We're getting close."

I can still see nothing but fog. How can he predict weather a day in advance in weather conditions like this? I can't see anything but uniform gray overhead. And neither can he. Would he know if a disaster were coming? I am sure that he would. He can smell danger. Or taste it or sense it in some other way. He is a good captain in these waters.

As I peer ahead through the shrouds of mist, we come out of the islands, back to the Peninsula itself. I hold my breath in awe. A mountain rises up from the sea. A sheer cliff of volcanic rock frames monster caves into which the waves break with a force that must shake the very roots of the trees at the top of the cliff. Spray and foam from the waves rise almost to the top of the cliff. The noise is deafening. The water at the base churns with a hundred riptides and cross currents in and out of the teasing, partially submerged rocks. And this is a *calm* sea.

I shrink back, drenched with spray. Johnny has slowed and is creeping closer. Over our heads the caves rise twenty, thirty feet. The sea howls and booms in and out of the cavernous mouths, one echo blending with the crash of the next wave. I look back at Johnny, frightened at being so close. My hands are frozen to the sides of the canoe, my feet braced in an instinctive attempt to stop its forward motion, as though I were driving a car.

Johnny is laughing in triumph, glorying in the sheer power of the display. He loves it, and he intends to give me the thrill of my life. I have always been timid, avoiding roller coasters and carnival rides of any description. I do not need physical danger for excitement. But now am given no choice. I hold my breath. I have never ridden the rapids, but it must be like this. It is insanity to take a large wooden canoe into that maelstrom, but I have no opportunity to protest. The sea engulfs us. The canoe shudders and buckets about, fighting the swells that drench and threaten to swamp us. The canoe groans. I hear it above the roar. I expect to see it snap in half at any moment.

We shoot free of the entrance and into the mouth of the biggest cave. Johnny is backing frantically and somehow we are turned around and facing forward as we shoot out again at terrifying speed with the backwash. It takes only moments, but I feel it all in slow motion as if in a life-threatening trauma. We hang, forever suspended, inches above a watery grave. I marvel at Johnny's skill as his strength and cunning fight us free of the rocks. When we are again in relatively calm water I cannot believe it is over. I am still in shock. My fear explodes into anger.

"Don't you ever scare me like that again! There's real danger enough without manufacturing cheap thrills!"

He has at least stopped laughing. I am shaking uncontrollably, and I must look like the ghost I almost became. Relief comes flooding back and with it comes cold and nausea and tears.

"My ancestors have been doing that for centuries," he says defensively. "I have to do it every so often just to keep my hand in. You don't want the old skills to die out, do you?"

"Why would anyone in their right mind want to go in there in the first place?"

"The hair seals. They used to live in the caves. We hunted them. They're all gone now. And you're right, I don't have to do that. But I need the challenge to keep my skills sharp. You were in no real danger with me."

"And what if something had changed that you weren't aware of? Like a landslide or a change in the currents because of the sea floor changing?"

He shrugs. "Those risks are all programmed in. I can handle it. Part of the trick is adjusting. Sensing where the danger is. There's no way you can predict everything the sea's going to throw at you. You ride with it. And you don't panic. My worth as a seaman is partly in not being afraid, not losing confidence. So lay off."

I collapse into the bottom of the canoe, drained of protest. Johnny is silent for a few strokes and then he begins a tale, his voice soothingly monotonous.

In the memory of my grandfather's grandfather, a hunting party from our village went into those caves after seals. There are ledges inside and the men had fastened their canoes and were killing seals with clubs, by torchlight.

This is not as one-sided a slaughter as you might imagine. Sometimes the seals won. They can retreat under water in seconds. You have to surprise them. It's black inside those caves. The ledges are narrow and slippery with moss and seal excrement and blood. The waves crash constantly around you. Torches smoke and falter and sometimes go out in the spray. And enraged bull seals guarding their families roar and bite and slash with flippers and tails. The men had clubs and only two hands to hold torches and hang on the ledge to keep from being knocked into the icy water.

On this particular occasion, the hunt was going well and the ledges were strewn with seal carcasses. The men were exulting and anticipating the praise such a large catch would bring in the village that night. Then a torch carrier at the cave entrance shattered their excitement with the most dreaded cry in their world:

"Enemy canoes!!"

The silent men watched in horror as a large war party of painted northern canoes came around the point, bristling with spears, and full of warriors yelling triumphantly at their unexpected advantage.

Our men were trapped. The enemy had cut off the channel that led back to the village and to reinforcements. The only escape was by sea and there was no time to launch canoes. The enemy quickly ringed the entrance to the caves. There were four of the northern canoes to each of ours. As long as our men stayed inside the caves they would be safe, but if they ventured out they would be butchered. The hunters had become the hunted.

It grew dark and cold and the tide rose. The men shivered miserably as the torches burned down and one by one went out. The smell of death around them sapped their courage. Quietly they discussed their desperate situation. The sea outside the cave mouth was negotiable only by high tide, and was suicide in the dark. The enemy had set up camp on the big island nearby; the men could see the fires blazing from their cold, dark, precarious perch. Lookout canoes maintained the night watch of the caves. A shout would bring the whole force down on a luckless escapee. The bluff above the caves was impossible to climb. Anyone attempting it in the daylight would be speared with ease from one of the canoes.

The siege went on for two days, the men in the caves becoming more desperate by the hour, weakened by exposure and lack of sleep and fresh water. It would not be long before they would be too weak to defend themselves when the enemy attack came.

One young man in the party waited until the dark of the second night, then quietly slipped out of the cave and began to climb the cliff. He was weak but he was young, and he was the only hope left to all of them. Behind him in the cave, clinging to the wet ledges, were the men of his family, and his neighbors whom he had known and loved and hunted with all his life, their lives dependent on his strength and his luck.

His flesh was numb with cold. The rock face was worn smooth and slippery from the constant assault of the waves. There were no ledges or cracks even for bird nesting. Here and there patches of moss and slippery lichen clutched the glassy surface. The young man clung where it was impossible to cling. He inched upwards where progress was unimaginable, and sideways where it was in fact, impossible. Inches of rock at a time were slowly, tortuously scaled. In the blackness of the night, the bated breath of the trapped men below held back time as they anticipated the sound of a body falling into the sea. But it did not come.

Cold sweat from tension and superhuman exertion made the young man's groping fingers, and toes, and his clinging body slippery. But sometimes the combined moisture of his body and the rock created a tiny suction. It was hardly enough to counteract gravity, but he used every advantage he could get. Weariness and dizziness overcame

135

him only when the smoothest stretch of water-splashed rock lay behind him. He rested briefly, his fingers wedged into a vertical crack.

Then he attacked the assault with hope-sharpened vigor. The night swam and sang beneath him, around him. He was a snail, a slug creeping vertically up the cliff. Consciousness came and went, but still he hung there, and still he crept upward. It was almost dawn before he realized that he had made it. He was at the top and the worst of his suffering was over.

Then he staggered up and struggled through the forest fifteen miles to the village on the other side where, before he collapsed, he told his tribe about his comrade's plight.

The villagers launched a war party of their own and came around the point, surprising the enemy in turn and routing them totally. The rescued men came out to join in the battle.

Johnny's voice ceases, and the only sound is the roaring of the waves against the cliff behind us. I am looking up at this cliff he has been describing. Only a fly could climb it. Maybe rock climbers with modern professional equipment could make it, in the daylight in teams, but for one man, naked in the darkness with nothing but his desperation, it seems a superhuman task. Unbelievable.

"Is that story true?" I demand.

"As true as anything you read in your history books. Legends are the history in an oral tradition. Besides, an Indian doesn't lie. It's true. He rarely has to lie. He just doesn't volunteer. He has passive resistance down to a fine art. You'd be surprised how easy that is. People don't ask him the right question, or he will deliberately misunderstand you, or he may even redecorate the truth, edit it a trifle to make it more artistic. Or merely interpret the facts uniquely. Or even tease you if he likes you. But out and out lying shows a lack of imagination and few Native Americans can be accused of a shortage of imagination."

"But how could you know so much about that story? Surely all that detail about climbing the rock is not in the legend!"

"I'm a good story teller, but you're right. I cannot tell a lie. I know about it because I tried climbing it myself once."

"Tell me!"

"I have always had something to prove. I had to see if I could do it. I am here to tell it because I cheated and used a rope. It can't be done otherwise. And yet he did it. He did the impossible to save his tribe and become a hero. And the other boy died alone on Pinnacle Rock. Why should one succeed and not the other? Why was one man's daring rewarded and the other's punished?"

"You want a moral? I'll give you a white man's moral. It's all in the motive of the climber. The one boy was challenging the gods for his own glory. 'Hubris,' I think the Greeks called it. The other one was concerned for his people. He climbed with the spirits' help and permission.

Johnny is quiet, thinking about that one. Finally, he points ahead of us. "The Island of the Whales," he announces. A large island emerges whalelike from the fog.

"My tribe traditionally camped on it in the summer so we could keep a full-time watch for whales and schools of salmon. The men kept their boats ready to launch at the first sighting, and the women dried and smoked the catch for winter use. Your people built a lighthouse on it when their sailing ships first began to use the strait regularly. It's a tiny island, no more than a large volcanic rock, really. Two caves run the length of the island, lava tubes. The tide goes straight through them. A big wave can shake the island. In the winter, storms make it uninhabitable. A small boat can't land on it in a heavy sea."

"It must have been lonely camping out here."

"Not really. There were several families there at a time and a lot of running back and forth to the camps along the shore, down by the dig and north of here. Summer was a social time, for visiting friends and relatives and catching up on gossip after the winter isolation."

"How does your tribe feel about your traditional camp and what you are trying to do?"

"Curious. Amused. Pleased, maybe, some of them; but most of them just don't think about it one way or another. They would care more if it had something to do with the sea and fishing. That's their world. And I make the women nervous, wanting to go back to a time without central heating and refrigerators. They're afraid it might catch on. No. I'm a crazy man. Education has made me weird. I'm out there all alone.

"I want to do it for them, but it is frustrating. I have done everything I know how to do. You say my motives are right, but there still doesn't seem to be any way down off that rock."

"You need help. A little of what the Greek dramatists called 'deus ex machina.' A god to come carry you off on his back."

"If you could arrange it, that would be most helpful."

"I'll see what I can do. I have problems of my own just now."

Johnny beaches the canoe on the tiny landing beach among submerged rocks that, even in the fairest weather, must make landing perilous to anything but a tiny boat. I crawl out of the canoe, miserable either in or out of it. I feel like a half-drowned kitten, and I probably resemble one. In spite of Johnny's efforts to entertain me, somewhere on this coast, in these waters, all motivation, all drive, all sensation other than misery have been beaten out of me. Emotionally, I am battered, bruised beyond my tolerance to respond. I sit huddled on a driftwood log and stare at the fuzzy gray fog world beyond the eternal dampness. Johnny prowls restlessly up and down the tiny beach, glancing occasionally at me. His helplessness to deal with me is obvious. At this point Richard would have had a temper tantrum. Johnny does not know what to do and indecision does not become him.

He collects driftwood in his prowling and builds a fire. He makes me more of the pine-needle tea. I hold it listlessly, for its warmth. I am so tired I cannot stay awake. I get one of the sleeping skins from the canoe and curl up on the sand in the lee of a driftwood log and sleep.

The hallway is foreshortened, perfunctory, almost unconvincing. Its menace is diminished by the forewarning of horror ahead. The staircase looms almost immediately. Relentlessly, my feet descend. I am helpless before their progress. One slow step at a time, prolonging the agony. My entire being screams for my forward motion to halt but it is no use. My gears are stripped, my brakes useless. I go on. My foot touches the spring. I fight against looking up as the door creaks open before me, but it is like fighting against time, or against vomiting, or against childbirth. The process has possession of me. I have no control.

She swings gently in the airless room, trailed by a faint cloud of dust. Dust lies matted over her shroud. The arcs she describes through the air increase slowly, as though a phantom wind has strengthened, but it is chokingly still. The silent, stiff mummy swings from its rope, higher and higher, closer and closer to me. I am held, unable to back away from it. My arms shield my face, but it is useless. The threadbare grain of the dust-stiffened shroud is magnified before my eyes, mercifully blotting out the staring eyes, and the shape of her hideous scream. And then the thing retreats, back, back, teasing, torturing, and then catches and comes straight for me, fast and hard. I close my eyes and it is upon me.

The force of the blow frees the hanging corpse and we fall together, the hideous thing on top of me, smothering me, choking me with dust and fear.

"Ruth, stop! Wake up, you're dreaming again!" The voice is familiar. It is Johnny's voice, reaching through my terror. I open my eyes, searching for the reassurance of a living, loving face, and stare at the fleshless, grinning skull of the dead, triumphant astride me.

I scream and lose consciousness, sinking into blissful darkness without shadows. When I come slowly up through the tunnel of consciousness again, I hear Johnny's anxious voice.

"Ruth? Can you hear me? Please, say something to me! Dammit!"

I am afraid to open my eyes. It might be another trick. Eyes closed tightly, I reach up, and touch reassuring flesh. My eyes open hopefully. It is Johnny. The nightmare is over.

"Was it the same dream?" Johnny asks.

"Only worse!! You!..."

I cannot finish the explanation. He pulls me over to the fire and goes for more wood.

I feel him stiffen with alarm from a distance of several yards. He comes down the beach at a run, all indecision swept away. I can see no reason for his urgency, but I do not question it. I climb back into the canoe. He covers the fire and launches the canoe faster than I would have thought possible. I can still see no reason for our haste. It is eerie. Impossibly, I think of enemy canoes stalking us through the fog. I want to ask, but I am afraid that silence might be a condition of our safety. I lie still in the bottom of the boat, wrapping a sleeping fur around me.

The fog seems thinner, and it is cold. I watch Johnny's long powerful strokes send the canoe through the water at racing speed. The set of his jaw muscles tells me what is happening. The storm he predicted earlier has sneaked up on us in the fog. Distracted by his concern for me, Johnny has misjudged its speed. It could be a fatal miscalculation.

The swells are larger, and the roar from the caves has increased. The sound of the swells hitting that wall of rock follows us a long way. I can imagine the wildness of the scene building up there, as the force of the Pacific begins to gather and smash itself against the land. Johnny's paddle thrusts are steady, the desperate tension of his shoulders controls his haste, disciplines his fear. If Johnny is afraid, our situation is truly perilous.

The wind is up and gusting now. The swells consistently increase in size. Whitecaps break around us. Foam begins to fly. Or is it rain, or both?

The swells have become mountains. We rise up their slippery slopes, poise dizzyingly on the edge, blinded by foam, until with a sickening plunge we are swallowed by the trough. I look up at the glassy skyscrapers of black water rising around us and wonder when we will be swallowed completely into the belly of the sea. Here, truly, lies the Valley of the Shadow of Death, between two mountain walls of moving water.

Water is everywhere, inside the boat, outside the boat. The sky and ocean are blending. We scud before the wind like helpless foam. I reach around and find a cup, and begin to bail out the deepening puddle of water I am sitting in. It is something I can do to help, to shut out the sight of tons of water poised over my head. This is not the end I had expected. I am not ready for my death. To drown in a storm at sea seems unreasonable, untimely. I have too much to do, too much ahead of me. My life is just beginning, not ending. Again I scream "unfair," my voice lost, blending with the wind's own scream.

My anger outgrows my fear. Desperately I bail, determined to do what little I can to save us. It seems futile, like emptying the sea with a spoon. Water is everywhere. I cannot tell where it begins and ends. We seem to be inside the ocean itself, moving within it. But we continue to move. I do not look at Johnny again. I would not be able to see him, as close as he is, and I could not stand that. I just keep up a steady rhythm of bailing, lifting the wooden cup mechanically and emptying it over the side where the ocean should be, like a child playing in its bath. I expect to feel the ocean claim me at any moment. The rise and fall are all slow motion now and it goes on forever.

Still, the hardness of cedar log remains beneath me. Still, we seem to move forward with the wind. I increase the tempo of my movements, I am beyond desperation, beyond my capacity. Hope pierces the watery blackness around me, born of the postponement of disaster. Perhaps Johnny can do it. If anyone can do it, Johnny will keep us alive. I should have faith in him and in the canoe, a tool that has survived hundreds, maybe thousands, of similar storms through time itself. The spirit of the cedar remains, strong and tough beneath me, the only remnant of safety, of solid reality I can cling to.

Half my lifetime later, long past believing, far beyond endurance, but finally, a shudder shakes the boat, a scraping. I am sure the end has come. Johnny is standing beside me, beside the canoe, sliding it up onto shore. We have landed.

Safety seems unreal. The imminence of death was reality. I stare at the rain-swept beach, the sheltered little cove, uncomprehendingly. Johnny is trying to pull the canoe up and out of reach of the waves. I can see that he is exhausted. He can hardly move the boat. He staggers. Johnny, the strong one. I am shocked out of my immobility. I scramble out of the canoe and try to help. Between us we manage to fasten the canoe to a log above the tide line. Only then we look around us.

My voice startles me. "Where are we?"

"I'm not sure. It looks familiar. Wait! Oh shit."

I look where he is looking. I see nothing but a grove of half-dead trees and, beyond them, a cedar forest rising.

"You know that island I told you about? The one that isn't supposed to exist? Welcome to the Island of the Dead."

"This? No. Not now. It's too much."

"Of course. It all makes sense. The storm. You were meant to come here. You're the first non-Indian to ever land here."

"That's no comfort. I don't want to be here."

"Would you rather be out there? We damned near drowned. We were lucky to land at all. I wonder what we're supposed to do next?"

"Build a fire and get dry, if that's possible."

"Yes, of course."

Johnny slowly gathers wood and I try to help. There is no shelter here, but the wind has abated some and it is no longer raining. Johnny finds enough dry wood to catch. No flame has ever looked as good. I huddle over it while he stockpiles wood. Daylight has slipped away in the storm. It is darker each moment.

"Now what?" Johnny murmurs, looking around.

"I don't care, just so you stick around. Don't get out of my sight."

Johnny is looking at me speculatively. "That may be the trick," he says. "You are supposed to be here, not me. It's not my trip. I am only the boatman. Whatever is supposed to happen here will happen to you, not me. You should be alone."

"No! Absolutely not. Never."

"I don't think we have a choice. I have to leave one way or another. You don't want me to leave permanently, do you? You want the dreams to stop? You want your questions answered, your fears released? That's what this is all about."

"How do you know that? And where would you go anyway?"

"Back to the mainland." He gestures. "The storm is over."

It is. The sea is calm. A faint moon and some reluctant stars have appeared.

"I don't believe this. You are proposing to leave me here in this graveyard alone all night?"

"I don't think you'll be alone. Besides, you have spirit protection," he continues hurriedly. "Otherwise you would not be here. No. I am sure of it. I have to leave."

"You're afraid to stay!"

"Damned right. But I would stay if I thought I should."

"You'll never come back for me. I'll die alone here! Johnny?!!" I am desperate.

"Courage. Face it. Bring an end to the dreams."

"Why me?" Why me, indeed. I have asked that question a lot, lately. I do not fight too hard to keep him. I have no fight left. I know Johnny is right.

SIXTEEN

I am alone. Totally alone on this Island of the Dead. Whatever happens I must deal with it myself. I have always gone from one man's protective circle to another's. But, from the first, Johnny has deliberately removed his strength from under me, leaving me to fend for myself. It is unfair. I have been custom-fitted for dependency; that is what men find attractive about me. I do not fight them. I adapt. I accept their leadership. I am trained to be half of a pair, what a man needs to complete himself. I am specialized. And in return, a man is supposed to be there when I need him. In reality, one never is. A man's protection is always an illusion.

Johnny's protection is no longer even an illusion. He has fled this place with indecent haste, abandoning me to my fate. All I have to do is stay awake, tend the fire, and he will come in the morning to fetch me. So simple. Just one night. How long can a night last?

As he left, he said seriously, "Stay alive, and stay sane." A small task. What threats to my life and sanity can there be on this tiny island? All the inhabitants are dead, except for the little creatures, the birds and rodents and insects that prey on the dead, and each other. There might possibly be a larger predator, but I doubt it. That isn't the threat, or the test. It is not the living I have to fear this night.

Darkness hoods the campfire, closing it off from the trees and the beach. The ocean seems a vast desert with ghostly waves echoing behind me. I refuse to leave the fire. There is wood enough to keep it going all night and I intend to stay awake to do just that. I wonder what lies beyond the trees that line the beach, but I will not venture into the darkness to find out. I will stay here beside the sea and deal with whatever comes out of the woods to seek me.

Johnny, in his haste, has forgotten to leave me water. I am thirsty, but I dare not leave the circle of light to look for water. Perhaps there will be fog, dew toward morning. That will have to suffice. I stare fixedly into the fire until the smoke rising and the shapes of the shadows begin to dance around me. Was that a movement I saw or merely the firelight flickering on the trees?

The normal deep woods night noises begin. I recognize the night birds, the crickets, small rustlings of nocturnal animals going about the processes of living. I have grown accustomed to these in my life with Johnny. Their domesticity should calm and reassure me. Their absence would be cause for concern. But I am not reassured. An owl's hunting shriek in the nearby trees sets me shaking. It is no use. The only thing that will calm me in this alien place is Johnny's arms. And he has left me here. Alone.

What do they want of me? I am only a woman. And an aging one at that! It is not necessary for me to be brave; I do not have to hunt big game, do battle with the enemy, or even deal with robbers, muggers, or rapists. I faced that fear, was it only the other day? And it proved empty. I reared my children successfully around all the pitfalls of modern civilization. Why try me now? All that should be left for me is to come to terms with death, step by merciless step, burying one after another of loved ones from my childhood, coming ever closer to my own mortality.

I admit to being a coward; I have always admitted it. I have my share of fears. But I have never been afraid to do what life expected of me. Is that not enough? I faced the challenges of a normal life. I married, had children, friends. I risked the ruin of my public image when I dared to come away with Johnny. Why must my courage be tested again?

The wind answers me. It moans through the trees. The cold breath of the waves blows through the fleeting warmth of the fire. I put on more wood. This is a different kind of test, requiring a different kind of courage. I have never faced *myself*. Myself, the enemy? It seems a strange and foreign place for me to find myself. On a tiny island of cedar trees in a cold and unfamiliar sea. If I were seeking myself I should go to my own source, back to the cornfields of the Middle West, to my heartland, to my own graves, my own ghosts. Why here, amidst the dead of a primitive race with whom I have no kinship or blood ties whatsoever? But what does it matter? My kinsmen are buried in even stranger places. Spirits recognize no skin color, or place on this earth. That makes sense. Little else around me does.

No matter how large or how hot the fire, it gives less and less warmth. Or else I grow numb. The cannoning of the waves has dulled to a drumbeat. The brilliance of the firelight and its contrast to the darkness dims. I am afraid I might be falling asleep, but I am not relaxed. I am still tense and fighting. No, something strange is happening around me. I fight it like an illness but relentlessly the colors bleed out of the night and I pass into a shadow state, beyond rest, beyond reality. It is beginning.

A log falls, and the fire blazes up. By its light I see the cedar trees rising around me, roofing me in, enclosing me. They no longer grow freely as trees; they have been tamed into a rough shelter. A shelter without comfort, more like a tomb. They form a long room with a sandy floor and a fire in its center. Smoke drifts up to escape through large cracks between the boards that form the roof. It is like Johnny's longhouse but much larger. And older and colder. Monstrously cold. I cannot feel the heat of the fire at all. The beating of the waves amplifies to fill my ears, my head. It occupies me. Or is it a drum after all?

Darkness wraps me in layers of deep brown velvet. A spark flares and its golden glow plays upon the layers of brown velvet wrappings with the fire inside, but without warmth, only glow, and the glow fades until it is suffocatingly dark again, the darkness of the hastily buried.

But this darkness is not still. Phantom breezes flutter massive cobwebs. Old skins creak and groan in a wind that does not freshen. Storms rage inside and out. The darkness is woven of a strange tapestry of smoky cooking fires and fish grease and spruce roots and marsh grass. It forms a harsh, threaded existence of simple priorities, of hasty pleasure, of deep abiding pain. The way things were. Alien, but tauntingly familiar. Images come to the edges of my awareness.

A face appears inches from my own, a hideous apparition, as ancient as man on this planet, as fresh as last night's nightmare. The scream dies stillborn on my lips as I recognize that it is a mask. There are others. Shadowy figures circle me, whirling in the darkness to present the full confrontation of their masks, too close. I try to count them, to order them, but it is impossible. They blend one into the other, each different, belonging to the family of fears.

A raven glides past, a bear shuffles heavily out of the blackness, a cougar prowls; a wolf, or is it a dog, stalks me? An elk dances teasingly by. My elk? Strange noises trace their paths. I recognize these masks as museum pieces, symbols of Johnny's tribal heritage. It is only fitting that they should be here. They, but not I. They mean nothing to me. Then why do they haunt me?

They are masks of fears; totems, and charms against fears. Old fears, someone else's cast off fears. They do not fit me. Then why do I chill with each new confrontation? Bugaboos in the night. Haunts, spooks, Halloween masks from far away pagan rituals. In my own heritage people used masks. Does my fear go back that far?

This is only playacting! I do not need these crude imitation beasts! I have gone beyond mere pretend; I have been the elk! I have worn his skin. The masks are nothing to me. I do not fear their living creatures, or the transformation of one form to another.

It is not death that I need fear in this place where everything is dead. It is something powerful enough to survive the process of dying and to thrive in the Spirit World. A new mask emerges. It is neither human nor beast, but born of both.

It is Hamatsa, Cannibal Man, who lives in the depth of us all! I cower before him. I must escape, but the drumbeat holds me, suspended in its web. I must break through it and flee. Beyond the terror of the mask looms the door. The mask seizes me. It whirls me in caricature of dance. I struggle; I whimper and cry out. He teases, taunts, whirling me ever closer to the door, then flinging me back out of its reach.

I am furious with him and with myself. Again, I am ashamed of my cowardice. He is a bully and therefore a coward also. If only I were stronger! We are the only two who are alive in this place. He is older than I and stronger. Or is he? He only lives as long as my fear gives him life. He feeds upon that fear. Without it he is helpless!

"Stop!" I cry in triumph. "I do not fear you. I know your name. You are Hamatsa, my servant. You are part of my strength, but not my master."

The drumbeat falls silent. The dancers move toward a long table that has appeared in the center of the room. People sit on the floor around it. It is covered with dishes of food. I am ravenously hungry and the food looks and smells delicious. I try to sit down with the others to eat, but I am pushed roughly away. The people at the table laugh at me and take turns pushing me.

The last push sends me stumbling to the stairway that leads to the door. I am desolate, shut off from the feast, the warmth, and the laughter. I am doomed to misery and I sink down inside myself into despair. And there I find anger. Deep, rich, satisfying anger. I breathe it in, in shuddering lungfuls, forcing out all the self pity and loathing.

Very well, if this is my fate, so be it. I march down the steps on strong legs, body erect, head held high. "Bring her on," I cry. "Do your worst. I am not afraid. I can choose not to be afraid. I am strong. I will fight these demons."

As I reach the door, it dissolves. It is not a heavy wooden door, but a tissue curtain, a membrane. I push through the membrane effortlessly to find myself inside the room of my nightmare. On the floor lie torn wrappings, stripped from the mummy casing. And sitting in the center of the discarded shroud is a little girl, a beautiful child. She smiles up at me and my anger dissolves. She holds up her arms and I lift her up and hold her close and a peace and security more complete than I have ever known envelopes the two of us. I want to stay here like this forever, but the child is stirring, restlessly shifting and changing, merging. She has become me, older, but a me transformed. I look at my hands and my body and exclaim. I glow with a golden light and from my fingertips flow beautiful colors forming shapes that dance gracefully around me.

I must show those people outside the room this miracle. I seem to float up the stairs. I am now welcome and a place is made for me at the table. But still I cannot join them, something prevents me. It is the heavy mask I am wearing. I must shed it first. Where has it come from? It does not belong to me. It is beautiful, inlaid with turquoise, decorated with blossoms, topped by a crown of triumphant sprouts. A fertility mask? I have given birth many times, why must I wear this encumbrance? It is a different sort of birth I must participate in now, a more fundamental one.

I am Seed and my path is the Way that all seeds before me have taken. I rest suspended in the darkness, peaceful, free from impatience. Inside me lies a promise, a dry expectancy, and my pattern. Within me is the subtle change, the difference that is me, whose time has come.

The blackness stirs around me, electrically charged. I yearn for warmth, the herald of light, and towards the blessing of moisture. Water touches me with its tingling strength. Its power blends with the deferred light. It courses through my dryness, charging, changing, energizing, completing, fulfilling, and filling out the empty chambers of my being. I swell to bursting with the force touched off within me. I split; no longer able to contain its relentless strength. I am absorbed by it, sending roots deep into the earth to balance and feed me, reaching tendril upward, faster and faster, stretching toward the source of the energy. I break through the crust of earth into the light. The sky falls softly, misting around me.

I live. I am whole. Positive and negative balance within me to provide my strength. I am part of everything around me. I am part earth, part sky, part sea.

From the richness of my joy I grow upward in the dizzying light. Higher and higher, branching again and again, my lower limbs sweeping the earth, my crown seeking the sun. I am Cedar Tree, tallest of the tall, graceful, fragrant. I stand poised at the edge of a vast sea, my height wreathed with clouds.

The earth stirs, shattering my crystalline peace. Someone comes. I see a girl standing between my roots. She moves with strength and courage, but her touch is loving. Her eyes are lit with fires of imagination and fun. She wears a curious costume: tight jeans and a bright blue construction helmet with a peacock feather bound to it. Her grin is mischievous, irresistible.

The sky darkens, the wind whistles around us. There's a drum roll of thunder. The girl climbs into my lower branches and clings to me for protection. A monstrous shape blots out the sun. Its wings churn all beneath it, changing the order of things. There is a blinding flash. Lightning dances around me. A roar of sound rolls over me, bending me double. I know who has come. It is the Wind Spirit. I tremble before his wrath. Have I climbed too high? Reached too near the sun? My roots are shallow. They barely support my weight.

With a mighty bellow, Thunderbird claps his wings and the wind assaults me. I cling desperately, but it is no use. My roots lose their hold on the earth. Slowly, grandly, I fall, across the vast ocean. With a crash that echoes the thunder my crown falls to earth on a strange land beyond the sea. My root wheel rests on one continent, my topmost branches touch another. I feel footsteps along my trunk. It is the dark-eyed laughing girl. She leads a crowd of people across me to this new land.

When they have all reached land, the girl collects my tiny seed cones and plants them in the new soil. They sprout at once and grow tall. But they are not cedar tress at all; they are corn stalks, tassels waving bravely, fat ears of seeds forming as I watch, amazed.

The cold, deep ocean I bridge has turned colder, turned to ice. The ice spreads to the new land, frosting my branches. Quickly the girl and her followers harvest the corn and carry it with them as they flee from the spreading ice. I am carried along, as corn seed. All around us columns of ice rise up. The ice spreads rapidly, capturing and imprisoning great beasts. A giant ram paces before us, turns, and is frozen where he stands. We hurry past him. Beyond, the ice has formed into a door, a curiously shaped one, like a cave mouth. We enter quickly.

Inside is an immense room of ice. Overhead, imprisoned in the ice of the roof is a giant bird, whose wingspan would cover a valley. As we watch, its flesh and feathers fall away, leaving us standing beneath a canopy of bone. We rush on into the depths of the cavern. The walls of ice open suddenly onto a vast green valley. Far above us the ice is sealing out the sky as it spreads, closing us in under an opaque ceiling.

The wind storm passes, leaving me warm and safe. I am back inside the longhouse and, finally, safe inside myself. Now I can join the others at the table. I have earned my feast.

I eat my fill and then I rest. I am very tired. I sleep like a child, smiling and smiled upon.

SEVENTEEN

I wake up back in Johnny's camp with no recollection of his having brought me. It is over. I am but the husk that has contained my dream.

Johnny waits solemnly. I laugh at him.

"How did I get here?"

"I brought you. Next morning. As I promised. I couldn't wake you, but you seemed okay. You've been sleeping for two days. I am glad you finally woke up. I was beginning to get worried."

"In your place I'd have been raising hell around here trying to wake me up to find out what happened!"

He shrugs. "You needed rest. You weren't going anywhere. I had you back."

I hug him quickly to hide sudden tears. I am weak and vulnerable, and also ravenous. Johnny brings me soup. I bolt it down, ignoring the greasy scum that would have revolted me not so very long ago, in another lifetime. He has made herb tea, and between the two I feel revived.

"Don't you want to know what happened?"

"You'll tell me."

"Try and stop me! But it's hard to know where to begin. Was it only a dream? If it was, it was the Olympic version. Or the Hollywood epic version. Bigger than life, and profoundly disturbing."

"Bad disturbing or good disturbing?"

"Good. Mostly, but such a simple label doesn't do it justice."

I relate the vision as nearly as I can recall it, detail by detail. Just the telling of it exhausts me. I am even weaker than I thought.

Johnny's reaction is curious. Before I can finish, he is pacing back and forth, unable to contain his nervous excitement.

"Is that all?" he asks.

"Yes, as nearly as I can remember. It was so vivid, but I might have forgotten some details. What does it all mean?"

"What does it mean to you? Do you make sense of any part of it? How do you feel about it?"

"Good. Damned good. I was left with that feeling anyway. As though I had solved the great riddles of the universe."

"What riddles did you solve?"

"I have no idea other than my personal one. A resolution of my problems. I made it through the door. You know, the door in those dreams I had where the mummy was on the other side. Only she wasn't a mummy. She was a cocoon that held all that beauty inside me. The butterfly me, I guess. And it was a different kind of door. It was a curtain, a membrane. It was so nice on the other side. And I can go back. Anytime I want to. That was the promise. Back to the womb, you suppose? No. I don't think so. It wasn't like that. There was security, but it wasn't dependence. It was dynamic. It was all me; I was whole, complete. Unified for the first time. All the parts of me were together at once. All of my fear boiled down to my being afraid that I wasn't lovable! And I wasn't afraid anymore. That made me angry. And that made the difference. I found the love I've been looking for all my life. But it wasn't coming from outside me; I was giving it to myself. And I think I'm meant to be an artist. I always wanted to be but thought I had no talent. Now I'm going to try it. If the spirits say I'm meant to be an artist, then I will be one!"

"But were there other parts to the dream that had nothing to do with you?"

"Yes. I have to ask. Who is Hamatsa? I've never heard that name before."

Johnny is looking at me strangely. "Cannibal Man. You're not supposed to know his name. He represented a powerful force in our culture. He's the skeleton in our closet, I suppose you could say. He was the climax of every winter dance to scare the child in all of us."

"That makes sense. He represented a deep, dark horror inside me, too. Shame and fear, I think, of what I as a human am capable of, the ultimate taboo. Yes. There's a Cannibal Man in the past of every culture on earth, I think. And as for my not having the right to know his name, you're talking to a woman who "persuaded" a headless, legless corpse of an elk down off a mountain when you, a card-carrying, full-blooded Indian couldn't do it! Let's hear no more about what I should or should not know. Let's talk about what I do know."

Johnny grins. "Point taken. All right, what do you know? What about the girl?"

"The one in the hat? Funny child. I can't imagine what she was doing there. Maybe she was part of a riddle, in the same context as the longhouse and the masks. They were not personal, and yet they were. But she wasn't personal. She was maybe the only thing in there that wasn't. I just can't analyze it. Not yet. It is too fresh. I have no perspective. Later I'll assess it all."

"I don't understand it either, but I do know that the girl has something to do with my people. The cedar tree that you became was the one in my vision, but there are things in that dream that you can't know about. I don't want to explain yet. But I know they are important. I want you to tell it all to the Council."

"Your Tribal Council? Back in town? Me?"

"Yes. As soon as possible. In fact, we'll leave as soon as you feel able to travel."

"Oh, Johnny, I don't know! I would feel really stupid. Can't you tell them? I mean, if you feel it is all that important?"

"It is that important. And you have to do it. I couldn't remember everything. And it needs to be fresh from your memory, firsthand. Please, Ruth? You've come this far with me. You've become part of my vision. Finish it. Like killing the elk, you won't regret it."

How can I refuse? I agree to go. In the morning. I fall back asleep, exhausted. I sleep off and on for the rest of the day, and through the night, dreamless.

The next morning, I am much stronger. Johnny gives me more soup and hurries me onto the bike. "We can make the tide, so you can ride all the way. Sure you're up to this? It's a long ride and you seem so weak?"

"The sooner we get it over with, the better. Besides, I'll forget if we wait. I have a feeling I'll find the strength!"

The ride to town has surrealistic qualities. The landscape slips by in Technicolor frames. I observe it from my risky perch, not quite part of it. I cling to Johnny desperately, closing my eyes to fight off the vertigo. If I lose consciousness, I will fall off.

I am clinging to Johnny's back as a lifeline once again. Déjà vu, I think of the poor creature who started out on this journey, having been terrified out of her complacency. This time I am weak but whole. Whole for the first time in my life. Johnny has been my support through it. I owe him so much! I squeeze him impulsively. He pries one of my hands loose from his waist and kisses it. That little tenderness does it. The floodgates of long buried tears break loose and I am sobbing convulsively.

Johnny stops the cycle by the side of the road. He scrambles off, catching me as I fall, and lowers us both to the ground where we sit while I cry my heart out against his chest. I can feel his alarm, but I am helpless to reassure him until the reservoir is empty.

At last I hiccup and search for a handkerchief to wipe my nose. "I'm sorry," I manage.

"Why should you be sorry?" His tone is flat and ugly. "I'm the sorry one here. Look at you!" His fingers are exploring my ribcage; I have lost weight. "Your man is taking lousy care of you. You're almost skin and bones. I took a beautiful, healthy woman and reduced her to this half-starved creature, passing out from exhaustion, crying hysterically, almost too weak to hold onto me. I'm a brute! I don't deserve a good woman!"

"Johnny, no! You don't understand! It's just the opposite; you're the best thing that ever happened to me! You took an emotionally crippled wreck and put her back together again, better than new!"

"Then why are you crying, woman!"

"Because for so long I believed I was not lovable."

"What?!! Dammit Ruth, you are the most goddamned lovable woman I ever met! How could you not *know* that?"

"Because my childhood taught me to feel otherwise. But the dream showed me that was wrong."

"Jeezus, woman." Johnny is hugging me tightly. I can feel his anger on my behalf, and his relief that I am all right. This sets me off again. I had thought there could be no more tears. I was wrong.

Finally I am truly spent. Johnny is surveying me critically. "I'm okay now, I think. I'm sorry about your shirt." It is awfully wet. Johnny grins and strips it off.

"That's no problem; it's warm enough without it. But how am I going to get you to town in this condition?"

"I really think I'm all right. I needed to do that. And I don't know about your other women, I can only speak for myself, but you're the best damn man I ever knew, and the most *lovable*! How could *you* not *know* that!?"

Johnny grins. I have done it. I've pulled him up out of the blackness he'd fallen into.

"Johnny? Are you going to tell me about *her*?"

"No." He can see the hurt in my face.

"Okay, maybe sometime. Not today. That's enough crying. We've got business in town."

We get back on the cycle. For insurance, Johnny ties me to him with a spare shirt from the saddlebag. We make the rest of the trip safely, Johnny's wet shirt flapping itself dry behind us. For part of the trip, I am musing about what other women have done to him.

Suddenly I am alert and aware, conscious that we are nearing the town. I look around me with renewed interest. The land is flat, former tideland probably. A small river runs alongside the road. Cattle graze, and a few horses. Peace. It is overwhelmingly peaceful. There are no fences! Common pasture. No individually held plots of land. We drive over a cattle guard that has paths on both sides of it! A dog is using one, a barefoot girl on horseback the other.

"Doesn't that defeat the purpose?" I ask Johnny, pointing to the paths.

He laughs. "At least it discourages the dumber cows from wandering around downtown and getting clobbered by the tourists. And it prevents mass migrations."

We are into the settlement. On the surface it looks like the other small fishing resort towns up the coast. The difference is subtle, but it is there. Activity seems to center on the main street and several charter fishing docks. Tribal-owned motels and a tribal food cooperative give the street an exclusive tone. But something is missing.

"No taverns," Johnny yells back as we turn off down one of the side streets. "No alcohol sold on the res."

Plainly a different world. The residential section is painfully tidy. The houses are tiny, wooden, and roughly the same age. Though some need paint, most of them are in nautical trim, gear stowed, lined up in parade dress, lawns manicured to the quick, and eerily still. Nary dog nor child mars the order. From here the town looks abandoned. Except for the eyes, watching us.

The settlement is tingling with expectation. They are waiting for us. The windows are full of watchers. We pull up in front of one of the least painted, most used houses. Our welcoming committee is small but select, and has an inclination to giggle. Seven pair of small black eyes stare solemnly at us from just inside the open door. Their owners range in age from ten or eleven to a baby held by the oldest.

As I dismount, my knees buckle. Johnny has to catch me. He carries me in and dumps me on the couch in the living room. It is a very old couch, scratchy plush with bad springs. The TV blares and fades alarmingly. The water-and-smoke-stained ceiling swims in and out of focus. I cannot seem to hang onto consciousness for very long. We are here. I give up and pass out altogether.

Fainting on someone's couch does away with the formalities of introductions, but it has left me in rather an awkward state—I have no social existence. I come to in the midst of a crowd of kids who are watching TV and ignoring me altogether. I sit up. Johnny is not visible. I need to find a bathroom, which appears to be a major difficulty because I cannot get anyone to look at me. They seem to avoid me out of embarrassment or shyness, but not indifference. To corner one of the children and ask would be a burden on the one singled out. They all seem determined not to be approached.

All right. I opt for the simplest way out. I get up to find the bathroom for myself. A door leads into a hallway. I am elated. With any luck there will be a bathroom off the downstairs hall. There is. The door stands open and I duck in.

I am trying to remember when social shyness of such proportions was this familiar to me. I am lucky to have an indoor toilet. The image of going outside to a privy clicks into place. South Texas. My Mexican-American friends. It has been a long time since I have felt this far out of place. To encounter such a very old emotional experience here is totally disarming. Now I really feel disoriented, both as to time and place.

I return to my place on the couch as discreetly as possible. The woman of the house, in her early thirties maybe, and slightly overweight, has come in from wherever she has been hiding, flushed out by my wandering around her house. She is hovering on the edge of the room, unsure of her obligation to me. I smile at her reassuringly. She sits, unreassured.

I sense that my end of the couch is probably where she would be sitting if I were not here. Johnny has placed her in an impossible situation. She does not know what to do. I am an overwhelming burden. She feels she cannot live up to my expectations. She does not even know what those expectations are. This frustrates and angers her because she wants to do right by this guest, for Johnny, and for whatever kinship they share. But she feels that anything she may do will be inadequate. What can she feed me? Lunchtime must be fast approaching. I can feel her dilemma. But she does not feel my encouragement. What can I possibly say to her to make things right?

"It sure is nice to have indoor plumbing," I offer hopefully. "Johnny's camp doesn't have many comforts."

It works! I can feel her pleasure, her relief. "Would you like a cup of coffee?" She asks.

"Could I? Please. I haven't had coffee since I left Seattle. Johnny doesn't believe in such civilized poison."

She grins a little. "Or beer, or TV, or even electricity. I know." She leaves for the kitchen. I consider offering to accompany her but I am sure she would rather I was confined to the living room. Nevertheless, I feel I can do more good by trusting my instincts so I simply follow her into the kitchen and sit down in a chair at the cluttered table.

"Where is Johnny?" I ask.

"He went to see the chief and to arrange for a spirit dance," she says, heating water self-consciously. She has to rinse out a cup for me. She is nervous about the mess in the kitchen. In another minute she will be all upset again.

"It's nice to be able to sit in a proper chair," I observe quickly. "And drink out of a cup," I continue, as she spoons instant coffee into the one she just rinsed. I am batting one-thousand. I can feel it. I suddenly realize how important that is. Johnny, damn him, has dumped me here, an alien in the midst of the tribe. We could have gone to one of the motels on the main street, but he's brought me here, expecting this woman to treat me like family, like an insider. It's a compliment, I suppose, but it has implications. He knows that the majority of the tribe will look to my hostess for clues on how I am to be treated. If she accepts me, is comfortable with me, then they will be as well. I have to do this right.

"Johnny likes things the old way," She says. "We don't all agree with him." She pours boiling water into the cup and hands it to me. "You want milk or sugar?"

"No. Black is fine. It's great, in fact." I sip the liquid gratefully. "God that tastes good! Isn't it awful how dependent we get on this stuff. I missed it something fierce, especially at first."

"I couldn't get along without my coffee," she agrees.

"It's a lovely camp," I continue. "Johnny worked hard making it just right. I do appreciate it, but it's hard to get used to doing without things you take for granted."

"I've never seen it," she says slowly. "But I hear it's just like the old ones."

"Nothing is different than it was two-thousand years ago, except for his motorcycle."

"I couldn't live that way. My grandmother did when she was young, but when she got older she lived with us and she wouldn't go back to the old way for anything. Even when we had no money, she wouldn't go back to doing things the way she had before. It's all right for the men I guess, but it was hard on the women."

The younger children have tailed me into the kitchen. I am a bigger draw than the soap operas. A chubby toddler leans on my leg and lusts after my coffee. I give him a sip, but he does not like it.

"He likes milk and sugar," the woman smiles. "I spoil him. Darlene brought him to me when he was only a week old. She was my cousin. We grew up together. I guess I feel sorry for him."

"Where is his mother?"

"She ran off to California I hear. Johnny won't talk about her, and she don't write."

"Johnny? Is she related to him?"

"His wife. Darlene."

I look at the little one, calculating, as he reaches for her. He's two and a half, maybe three years old. "That makes this one Johnny's son?"

"Flint." She picks him up, shyly, careful not to look at me. I realize she has been trying to find a way to explain this to me from the beginning.

"Does Johnny have other children?" I ask.

"Just this one. Having one baby without a doctor was too much for Darlene. She was only eighteen. She had a hard time, I think. As soon as she could walk, she headed for town, carrying the baby. She brought him here to me and took off. She didn't say a word. She was scared. Her grandmother and her aunt died having babies. Johnny was crazy to make her have that baby by herself. He delivered it, and I think it scared him plenty too. He never talks about it."

I am silent, remembering the helplessness of being pregnant, the fear that something might go wrong, the terror of being stranded with no medical help, the possibility of bleeding to death. If Johnny had done that to me, I would never have forgiven him. He can be so understanding. And yet so stubborn. So lost in his obsession. Poor Darlene. Damn him!!

I realize that this woman, Darlene's cousin, is waiting. I am expected to say something. "That poor woman!!" I put all of my own dismay into my voice. "And poor baby! No wonder you spoil him. He's lucky to have you."

She smiles and actually looks at me. I have passed another test, been accepted into an even more exclusive club than Johnny. I'm one of the women.

I have a lot to think about. One part of me is fascinated by this new knowledge about Johnny, but another voice is nervously telling me to think about it later, to wait for a better time. Right now I have another priority.

Johnny and Jude's husband Jim arrive before the problem of lunch intrudes on our new comradeship. Johnny's presence seems to reassure Jude, as she is called, as mine never could. She goes about her normal activities, leaving my entertainment to Johnny. I will insist upon helping her, but first I pounce on Johnny. "When? And what's this about a spirit dance?"

Johnny grins. "Tonight you will dance your vision. I was lucky the salmon boats are all in. There's plenty of fish; my uncle just shot a deer. We're all set."

"I'll bake a cake," Jude offers. The significance of it occurs to me with a rush.

"This is going to be expensive!" I protest. "I'm sorry, I didn't real- ize. Will you have to give gifts, too?"

"I should. I am hoping to get by with refreshments because it's on such short notice. You're going to have to be the big gift, baby. If you're a hit, they'll forgive me!"

"Johnny!"

"Just kidding. You really are nervous aren't you?"

"What do you expect? Of course I am. And what do you mean I have to dance? You've got to be kidding! I have to be falling down drunk to lose my self-consciousness enough to waltz. I can't get up in front of your people and do some kind of freestyle interpretive dance! It's bad enough just making a speech. They're going to resent me no matter what I say. I don't belong here. I'm the enemy, remember?"

"Shit. What's important here? Your story or you?"

"You tell me. This was your idea."

"It won't be bad, Ruth. I promise. Just forget who you are and what you are and tell the story. Believe me, they will want to hear it! The dance is traditional, but hardly anybody does it anymore. They won't expect anything. Whatever you do will be just fine!"

He settles down with Jude's husband and the kids to watch the news, and I storm off into the kitchen to bother Jude, my female protestations dismissed. It is a different world, all right. But it sure has familiar chauvinistic overtones!

EIGHTEEN

Jude assigns me the task of baking the cake and sends Johnny to
the store with me to get a cake mix. I do not argue. I know she
wants me out of the way and I am glad to be with Johnny. I am so
nervous I cannot concentrate and am little help to her anyway.

Even though it is a short distance, we take the cycle. I am
relieved because I am still weak and need all my strength for tonight.
We are the center of attention as we pull onto the main street and
cruise down to a large, general store complex. News of the evening's
entertainment has spread. Johnny waves, smiles, and shouts at
dozens of people in cars and pickups and motorbikes. Only the
youngest and poorest seem to be on foot. Everybody who is anybody
has wheels of some description.

Johnny stops to talk to some buddies while I wander into the
grocery part of the store. It is a huge operation, apparently privately
owned, selling sporting goods and curios as well as drugs and groceries. It caters to the charter fishermen with resort prices, but it is
full of locals. The selection is large at least. I pick out two boxes of
cake mix assuming that everybody likes chocolate, and some sugar
for icing, and read the notices while I wait for Johnny to finish and
pay for the groceries. My purse is somewhere back at his camp. I
have not seen it in some time. The notice board offers pickups for sale
and displays a large and conspicuous bad-check list. A sign in red
announces "No checks cashed without approval of manager or two
pieces of ID. and place of employment."

A middle-aged white man with mean eyes is circulating through the store. He watches me with suspicion. I resent his assumptions. In his eyes I'm poor white trash at least, more likely one of those hippie types. Certainly sleeping with *one of them* and likely to shoplift, float a bad check, and commit all manners of atrocities against middle-class property owners and shopkeepers.

I repress a giggle at my new perspective. Not very long ago he would have assumed I was like him without thinking about it at all. Oh Johnny, my darling, what have you done to me? Johnny shows up finally to pay for my purchases. The WASP manager gives me a dirty look and takes the money. I feel as though I need a bath. I undoubtedly do need a bath. I have not thought about that either in some time.

"This isn't the only grocery in town?" I ask on the way out.

"There's the Tribal Co-op down the street, but nobody goes there."

"Of course not. Co-ops don't have the excitement of twentieth century merchandising. They don't make it fun to spend your money! I want to go anyway. Just to look around. Compare prices. I'm trying to get acclimated fast."

He shrugs. It is only a block away, deserted except for a bored, young matron behind the counter. There is little variety, no cake mixes at all, and prices are somewhat lower. I get a can of pop and check the notice boards on the way out. The difference here is astounding. These are filled with official federal job lists with classifications and requirements, notices of childbirth education classes, senior activity meetings, and one request for bids on a logging job offered by the Tribal Council, specifying that there would be a Native American preference. Also, there is one notice that credit will not be advanced on Charter Fishing Company vouchers, and a list of food stamp regulations.

I get back on the cycle shaking my head. "No customers. In spite of the rampant prejudice, everyone shops at the other place!"

"Not everyone. The older women get their staples at the co-op. And some of the younger ones, too, on welfare with lots of kids to feed."

Back at Jude's, lunch is spaghetti, salad with bottled dressing, and beer. I look at Johnny. He does not comment. Apparently there is some drinking done in private. With any kind of luck my audience tonight will not have to listen to me cold sober. Some of them may not even hear me. But the older ones, and the churchgoers, will not be drinking.

I eat and the food tastes strange, foreign. Have I changed that much, or is it just nerves? I do not dare touch the beer. I have pop with the kids. And more coffee. In my heightened sensitivity, alcohol might knock me out again. Which will not do, since I am tonight's star attraction.

At least Jude lets me help with the dishes. I frost the cake and have a nap. A hot bath and more coffee and I am as ready as I will ever be. We take the bike again, with Jude, Jim, and the kids, riding in a pickup. The evening is beginning to quicken. Excitement flares around us like Midwestern lightning bugs. The kids' eyes glow with it, and I flash hot and cold with tension.

The civic center is a new tribal hall not unlike the longhouse I have been getting used to. I am shocked by all the preparations. People are arriving by the truckloads. It is like a country fair, a church potluck supper, and a circus. They are all there. The whole tribe has gathered from the oldest to the newest and including the infirm. I do not know whether I am expected to be a revivalist preacher or a tightrope walker, but I am clearly expected to be the evening's entertainment. I feel way out of my depth, and terrified that I am going to say the wrong thing and offend somebody. Their careful non-stares run the gamut from curiosity, to doubt, to open hostility from some of the young adults. I turn from them to Johnny. I am shaking.

"Johnny! What do I say???"

"Take it easy, woman. This is no white speech. No lecture. They aren't going to take notes. Just say what you feel."

"That's what frightens me. What have they come for? What do they expect? What do they want me to say?"

"They don't know, but they'll know when they hear it if it's right. If it isn't, they'll know that too. They've been disappointed many times. You wouldn't be the first."

I survey the noisy crowd, gossiping and eating, the kids racing around having a good time. They are waiting. It is my move. My

dream has called them and I have to face them. And whatever powers made that call happen will just have to sustain me now. Johnny
promised it would be all right.

Johnny starts up to the front of the long room. I take a deep
breath and follow him. *Anywhere* I said. I never dreamed it would lead
here. Our progress is marked by a wave of silence. Polite, curious,
respectful silence. They will courteously allow me to make a fool of
myself. Even the children are still.

I suddenly feel oppressed by the heaviness of the room. I feel the
massive weight of all those felled trees, the heavy scent of freshly cut
cedar. The glare of electric light is a pale parody of ancient fires.
Mostly I feel the weight of all the black eyes that follow me in curious expectation.

Johnny's introduction is short and simple. "This is Ruth. She has
something to tell you that I think you will want to hear."

Damn him. My voice is weak, but determined. In the deep
silence it carries well. So well it startles me. It lends an air of detach-
ment, of unreality to an already unreal experience.

"I understand it is traditional for me to dance and chant my message. I hope you'll forgive my departure from custom on the basis of
my cultural deprivation. I'm having enough trouble telling this without choreographing it!"

Polite silence. Jeez. I grope on.

"It is difficult for me, an outsider, to intrude on your spiritual
lives. And I can't explain to you why, but I am involved somehow with your spirits. But, as I discovered recently, spirits have
no color and no race. The values of this world do not apply in the
other one."

There is a stir, a sighing like wind in the reeds, of recognition and
perhaps approval. Encouraged, I stumble on.

"When I came here, to the Peninsula, I was between lives; my
children are grown and I am not yet ready to die. I needed some kind
of spirit help, a direction. We all do.

"Soon after I came to live at Johnny's camp I began to have
nightmares. Terrible, frightening experiences that I hate to even think

about now. There were certain other signs, a cougar that came into camp and terrorized me, but left no tracks.

"Johnny couldn't find any trace of it, and it didn't take the meat that was left out. But it left a skull behind, a human skull that it dropped from the roof."

I can sense the quickening of interest. They are with me.

"The next day I found a second skull on the beach. Johnny said that it appeared to him that the spirits are restless and that they were trying to communicate with me. I didn't know whether I agreed with him or not, but I had to stop the nightmares, no matter what the cost."

My audience rustles their acceptance. Their expectation is palpable now. I want desperately to satisfy it. I would even make up something to make them happy, but all I can do is give them the truth. And they deserve no less.

I do not look at Johnny. I forget that he is here. I forget where I am. I am back in the longhouse in the trees on the Island of the Dead and the firelight is glowing dimly before me. I describe what I saw there, what happened to me, from the time we left Johnny's camp until I awoke back in that camp.

I am dimly aware that something strange has happened to my audience. I can almost pinpoint the place in the narrative where it happened. It is where I am describing the curious girl who walked the trunk of the cedar tree. There is an electrification of the atmosphere around me, but I close it out, absorbed with my vision. When I am finished, I look around for Johnny. He is standing beside me.

"Ruth," he says loudly for all to hear. "The girl that you described, the one with the hat. Do you know who she was?"

It is important. I think hard, and shake my head. "I have no idea."

"You've never seen her before, or her picture?"

I shake my head again.

"Has anyone ever mentioned the name Mayva Johns in your hearing before? Today or at any time before this?"

"Never. I can't remember ever hearing that name, and it's unusual enough that I'd probably remember it."

167

"Jude?" Johnny calls to our hostess in the back row. "Did you discuss Mayva with Ruth or in her hearing?"

"Not a word, so help me! It never came up. I didn't know it was going to."

Johnny continues. "I didn't know about Mayva myself until today when we came into town. And even if Ruth had heard about her, she could not have known about that hat! Those of you who need proof, I guess you've got it."

"What about a newspaper?" The question comes from a young man in the front. He has long hair and a sparse Oriental-appearing goatee.

I laugh. "I haven't seen a newspaper since I left Seattle. I forget what they look like."

Jude is shaking her head. "We don't have one and, besides, the story hasn't come out yet in any paper I've seen. We're not big news in Port Angeles."

"Ruth told me the whole thing, including the part about the girl yesterday back at camp before she could have seen any newspaper," Johnny says firmly.

"Johnny, what's this all about? What does this Mayva Johns have to do with me? . . . Is she the girl in my vision?"

"You sure described her. Down to that crazy hard hat she wore when she was just a kid."

"That's easy to settle. Where is she? I could probably identify her if I saw her again," I say reasonably. "Is she here?"

There is an uncomfortable silence.

"Mayva died in a car wreck night before last," Johnny explains.

My legs will no longer support me. They have been looking for an excuse to collapse for some time and they have found one. The room revolves crazily for a moment and everything is still.

NINETEEN

Consciousness comes back slowly about midday the next day. The TV finally penetrates the protective layers of sleep and the coming and going of children brings me out to face the day. When I realize where I am and what is expected of me, I want to go back into unconsciousness. But it is too late. Jude brings me some coffee and I am stuck with the living. I seem to have blanked out again. I cannot remember anything after Johnny's announcement. My weakness, no doubt. A charitable interpretation. I have some strange symptoms of weakness! First I see visions; next I will hear voices!

"Where's Johnny?" I ask Jude.

"He and Jim are down looking at Jim's boat. They should be back any minute. He said to let you sleep. I tried to keep the kids quiet, but. . . ."

"No problem. They couldn't have wakened me before I was ready, anyhow. Boy, do I need this coffee!"

"I can get you something to eat when you feel like it. You're supposed to meet with the Tribal Council this afternoon. Johnny said to tell you."

"Oh boy. I had better wake up fast. I'll fix myself an egg if you have one. I haven't had an egg. . . ."

"Sure. Come on in the kitchen."

I follow Jude into the kitchen. "Jude, what did you think about last night?"

"It's pretty weird, but there's a lot of weird things that happen. I wouldn't have paid much attention to it if it hadn't been for that part about Mayva! I guess I'm not the only one. You're the main topic of conversation in town today."

"What are people saying? And what happened last night after I passed out?"

"Not too much. Your passing out sort of put an end to the evening. Chief Jimmy Two Ravens calmed everybody down. He's old and in a wheelchair, but everybody listens to him. We all needed somebody to take charge, and to take the responsibility of interpreting what you said. He was all excited, which doesn't surprise anybody. He always talks about the Old Way and the legends. This is his kind of meat. Some of the others aren't so pleased."

"Who?"

"The church people, mainly. And some of the young ones. But one way and another you stirred the tribe up like a nest of wasps."

There is a disturbance in the living room that demands her attention, and Jude leaves me to my chagrin and my breakfast.

I have finished a civilized morning meal and am feeling much better about the world when Johnny strolls in.

"Are you ready to go?" he asks.

"Never. Sit down and have some coffee."

He does so.

"Johnny? What is going on?"

Johnny grins. "Not much. Just a major revolution."

"Forget it! Just because of the ravings of a neurotic woman?"

"You're a pawn, my love, like the rest of us. You came like a prophet bringing a message from another world, and now it's stand back and watch the fun!"

"Me, Moses, bringing down the tablets?"

"Very like. Except your tablets weren't quite as specific as his."

"What do they make of my dream?"

"An amazing number of conflicting theories! However, the chief will prevail. When the dust clears eventually, your old friend Johnny will very subtly lead his lost tribe into the Promised Land of the future. We will no longer be just a vanishing species, an archeological curiosity, but guardians of the hope of tomorrow."

"And what does all that mean?"

"Just be patient and listen. Your personal struggle is over. You are part of the audience now.

"It's simple. What your dream has brought the tribe is a tangible link with our own past. We are a race with deep ties to the Spirit World. We have never grasped the practicality of this in the white world. Our old people can tell the children the legends, but when the youngster goes to school and the teacher asks him to explain a vol-canic eruption, is he going to tell her the mountain gods were angry and threw rocks at each other? He knows better. Oh, the teacher might be understanding, but the rest of the kids would laugh.

"There has been no relevancy. The old people knew that it was important to remember, but they didn't understand why. The stories don't explain how to fill out a form to get food stamps. And no one will deny that food stamps are more efficient for putting dinner on the table than bows and arrows and even more efficient than guns and bullets. The difference is, there's no pride in cashing them in! And that's a helluva subtle concept for them to understand, let alone to change.

"I've sometimes caught a glimpse of the possible significance of our powers for the future of the human race, to fill in the gaps between the white man's understanding of the universe, but I could-n't communicate this to my people, or to yours. I was like that boy stranded on the rock. I was between worlds. You brought the con-nection, the bridge between the two."

"What connection?"

"Wait and see. It'll sound pretty far out. I don't buy it all, but that's not important. They do! They believe in its reality, in the com-ing to life of the legends, and in themselves and the importance of their past. It's an infusion of hope into our whole lifestyle. Now we can wait, and guard our powers like the secret of the cave, until the white man is ready to understand us."

"What cave? You mean the one in my dream?"

"Come. Let the chief explain."

Johnny and I walk into a meeting already in session. A knot of excited people clump at one end of the huge room. Their voices echo among the empty folding chairs. The artificial light seems even more unreal today. The windowless building should never be lit by anything but council fires. An expectant hush precedes our entrance.

I am introduced to the dominating figure, the white-haired man in the wheelchair with the frail appearance and the commanding voice whose name is Chief Jimmy Two Ravens; to Charlie Davids, a stocky young man padded with beer fat, with long hair and a wispy mandarin goatee; to Mrs. Blackstock, a prim, thin-lipped matron in a dark polyester pantsuit; and to Jennie Samson, a motherly type with flyaway white hair and a generous figure stiffly confined in a print housedress and run-down white nurse's oxfords. I smile at them all, sharing their nervousness.

"Are you feeling better, child?" The chief asks, his impatience barely concealed.

"Yes, thank you. Much better," I reply. "Is anybody else coming?"

"I think not. They are waiting. To see which way the elk jumps."

"I know how they feel. Dreams look different in the daylight."

"Yes. Yours seems to have survived the test of daylight and sobriety better than most. We were just discussing the significance of your vision to our tribe."

"I can see that the presence of Mayva in my dream gives it an emphasis it might not have had otherwise, but I fail to understand what it means for you. It was a personal dream and had personal meaning."

"There is message enough for all in your vision. It means one thing to you and something different for us. There is nothing unusual about that.

"The message that you bring is in the spirits' language, in signs and pictures that we must read. You can help us with your memory of it, but we must interpret. You cannot understand what you have seen."

"You are right about that. I certainly can't! I will help in any way that I can, of course. I am most interested to hear what you read in it."

"What you have brought us, child, is no less than a promise made to us by the Old Ones. A renewal of a prophecy in the old stories, which we chose not to believe. The Thunderbird's lost cave has teased our memories from within our legends for hundreds of years, maybe thousands. From the beginning.

"You describe a place, a true place, and the same one that the legends tell us is the cave of the Thunderbird. You describe in your own words the image of the great Thunderbird imprinted in the roof of the cave that is spoken of in the legends. This identifies it positively. You tell us more: that the cave lies beyond the frozen image of a giant ram. I know this place! I can point it out on a map! I have been there myself but did not know that the cave lay beyond. It was hidden from my eyes as it will be from others who would seek it without the personal guidance of the Thunderbird.

"I am an old man, and I wondered why I should live so long in this condition." He indicates his wheelchair scornfully. "But I understand now. I am here because I must hear this story and recognize this place that you describe. No one else would be able to point the way. And this gives me more pleasure than anything I have done in my lifetime.

"This happening is not for me. Or for you, my child. This is for my people, my tribe. And perhaps for all of the Indian nations. Our Spirits have spoken in a language that we can understand. After all these years of silence, they have spoken out to warn us and to guide us to a place of safety."

There are murmurs of disagreement at this point, but the old man ignores them.

"We were meant to find this place, and the time for us to find it was carefully chosen. Why now? It must be because the white conqueror is about to destroy himself. The Thunderbird's cave is meant to be a natural shelter against a holocaust to come. We have learned much from this white conqueror. We shall use his knowledge to survive him. We shall concentrate from now on to learn all that he can teach us about our world, but for purposes different from his own. He knows many of the secrets of the earth, except the most important secret of all. Respect. He does not respect that which he fancies he understands. We respect and revere the Life Force. Your race seeks to control the earth for its gain. And so your greed will destroy you. But you will not destroy us also.

"We will take back our earth, and care for it. You, Ruth, will lead us through your vision to our place of salvation, where we will wait for the earth to heal her wounds and prepare for our return. The Thunderbird promises!"

I am overwhelmed. Staggered. Johnny was right; I am suddenly a prophet! This has gotten completely out of hand. Surely these people are not buying my nonsense.

I am right. There are stirrings of rebellion. I wait for the others' dissent. Johnny has said that it is not my struggle.

"How do you know that this cave, if we find it, would be a shelter from some nuclear blast?" Charlie Davids asks.

"We cannot be sure until we have seen it, but the Spirits would not lead us there without purpose."

"But why should we believe the words of a white woman? Why should our Spirits speak through her? It is a false message!" Charlie Davids continues. I have to agree with him. We all look at the chief.

"This woman," he begins, pointing a bony shaking finger in my direction, "has been chosen to bring us a message because she was willing and able to listen. She believed and she listened when none of you remembered how. You have been slaves too long; your own spirits are dead in you. Mayva is our sign that the message is true and must be listened to.

He continues, "If Mayva herself had had the vision and told it to us, would her telling have made the impression upon you that this has done? No. It would have been discounted like all the rest of our vague warnings from the past have been. It took a white woman to make you listen to your own ghosts! She believes in what she has seen, and she represents the direction from which the danger to us will come. You believed Ruth's white ancestors when they told you your Spirits did not exist. Now believe her when she tells you they do exist!"

The old man looks commandingly at each of them in turn, and insists, "If Ruth is acceptable to the Spirits, I will not question her. I don't need Mayva's presence in her vision to convince me. There are too many other proofs. I have been waiting for such guidance for a very long time. I knew it would come, before it was too late for me."

His words still even my protests. I am uneasy about my role in all this, but I lack the conviction to oppose him. I am a pawn. I am being used! This clever old chief is using me to manipulate his people. He is in another world. He feels the spirits have spoken to him, to all of them, through me!

The rebellion of youth is not so easily extinguished. Charlie Davids has not given up. "Even if what you say is true, even if there is a cave and we find it, if this holocaust comes, how long would we have to stay there? How would we survive? What kind of a life would that be to live in a hole in the ice for years?"

The old man looks at Johnny. Johnny shrugs, and answers "It takes years for radiation to cool down sufficiently to be safe for humans, and it depends on how much there is. We'd need a Geiger counter to keep checking. This is all highly speculative. We don't know that any of it is possible. The first step is to find the cave and assess its possibilities, then see what we would need to survive there."

"Yes. Tell us again about the cave, Ruth. The ram. Where was he?" The chief's eyes are shining with delight.

"He was on a ledge. On this mountain, I guess. We were all escaping from the ice. The ice formed a mountain around us. The ram was turning around. I never saw one turn around like that. He had run out of ledge and so he backed his hind legs up the face of the cliff and was going to face the other direction when the ice froze him solid in that position. He was huge. Half as big as this room."

"I know that place!" The old man's excitement is contagious. "I have seen his hoof marks! Once as a young man I went too far while I was hunting. I was chased by a bear beyond the timberline onto a ledge of rock. I looked up at the hoof marks on the cliff behind me in wonder. They were twice my own height! I knew it was a spirit place! To be so close myself and not find it!" His voice is wistful.

"The prints were in the ice?" Charlie Davids asks him.

"No. In the rock itself," the chief answers. "It must have been only clay when he stepped on it and was frozen. But the prints are still there. I can show them to you!" He looks down at his useless legs and the wheelchair. "Or I could have when I was younger. But you can find them for yourselves. I will tell you where to look."

"Where was the cave in relation to the ram?" Johnny asks me.

"Beyond it. Above. The ram seemed to be a sentry, pacing up and down. The cave opening was very strange. Its shape, like a split in the rock, or ice, was very confusing. A fissure. I would imagine it would not be visible from above or below. It would be hard to find. Inside it opened up into a regular cave. Only it was monstrously big. The bird in the ceiling was two or three times the size of this building."

"You have all heard the legend that describes that bird!" the chief adds, triumphantly. The women murmur agreement.

"And beyond the cave? You described a valley?" Johnny asks.

"As though it were in the heart of the mountain. No. As though I had gone through the rim of a volcano and come out into the bowl in the center! Only the ice covered the bowl while I watched."

"White Hell Glacier." Charlie Davids' voice is full of awe. "It is impossible to cross!"

"But I didn't cross it. I was underneath it!"

"If there is a valley beneath the ice," Johnny says slowly, "as you describe it, perhaps where the warmth of the volcano has melted some of the glacier away from underneath; the ice above might make a decent filter to keep out radiation particles and still leave enough light and moisture to grow food. It is possible that it could form a natural bomb shelter, if all the conditions were right. Depends on how much ice would melt in the blast and how much radiation there would be to keep out."

"Who would go?" Jennie Samson finally breaks her timid silence to ask suspiciously.

"That depends on who is around when it happens, who wants to go, and who is capable of reaching it. That would all have to be decided at the time," Johnny continues.

"How would we live there?" Charlie Davids asks.

"You would have to prepare for a long siege," the chief answers him. "You would bring in seeds and animals enough to make your-selves self-sufficient for as long as it takes, as Ruth's vision indicates."

"It would be a difficult way of life," Johnny points out.

"And one we are not used to," Charlie Davids says, scornfully. "We are fishermen, harvesters of the sea, not the land. We would have to leave our ocean, which is our life. It has kept us unique all these years, barely touched by the white man's culture. In that valley we would have to become like white men—farmers. It is not our way."

"If the Lord wants us to survive, should we question His will?" Mrs. Blackstock contributes.

"If He means for us to have an ark and save mankind and the animals from destruction, we must do as He commands," Jennie Samson adds firmly.

The chief's rebuke is gentle but authoritative. "I think, ladies, that we are talking about something bigger than Christianity here. We are going beyond the white religion to our own source of power. The white man's god has no place in this."

"He is our God as well," the women chorus, almost as one.

"You were baptized by the white man in his religion, but you were born Indian," the chief continues in a gentle voice, which tempers the shock of his words. "Your blood and bones and flesh belong to another strength. And it is that strength that commands us to leave the sea finally and hide in the mountains until our world is returned to us.

"The white man's god is only a vague metaphysical notion, which is beyond human understanding. The missionaries tried to make us believe that our Spirits were like theirs. They failed to understand that our Thunderbird, who led Ruth to his cave in her vision, is a symbol for a very real power, a natural force you can see and feel and hear—the power of the wind and the storm. Our Spirits are real. Our people journey to the Spirit World as a white man would travel to another country on this earth. They are out of our sight as if they were in another country, and they are changed, as journeys change most people, but they are real still. Sometimes we can hear them and feel them and even see them. And we will all join them there."

The women are bristling, but obviously out of their depth theologically. I am fascinated.

"You mean they are in another dimension?" I ask, unable to stay out of the debate.

Charlie Davids answers me scornfully. "Can you see the wind? Can you see electricity? Can you see the force pushing the waves or forcing the mountains to split apart? No. You can only see the path that the force leaves behind it. But you know the force is there. You can even measure it. You call what you can measure real. Spirit energy could be measured also if you had the instruments."

Johnny interrupts. "This is no time for a philosophical debate. Leave that to the ones who come after, to interpret what we have done. Ruth has felt the force of the Spirits' energy. She believes. We all know it exists. The white man does not, in spite of the evidence. But he is learning. Give him another century or two; if he survives, he might begin to appreciate what we have known all along and he has forgotten."

"And if our conquerors destroy themselves, we must seek shelter where our Spirits have led us," the chief continues smoothly. "When it is over, the world will recover. Even if it is changed, it will be ours to repair and renew. Because we are the guardians of the true source of power, of energy. We respect it. The earth changes as seasons change; spring comes again after the winter. If we must change also, then let it be as the Spirits dictate. The first law of human existence is survival. If we must first hibernate as the bear, we shall do so. Our conquerors will vanish in their own smoke, and we will pick up the scattered remains of our lifestyle. And we will remember the lessons they taught us. We cannot ignore what has been given us. We must accept this shelter like a gift from the tides.

"I know it is difficult to understand, and it is difficult to change," the chief continues. "But when the disaster does come, all of us here may be gone. I do not hope to see it myself. I could never reach our place of safety in this," he indicates his wheelchair again. "You may all squabble like gulls over a fish head, but I do not doubt that when the time comes, your children will choose life over death, and it is our duty to give them that choice."

The doubters are silent. For now. Recognizing his temporary victory, the chief looks at Johnny and Charlie Davids. "Are you then convinced in your hearts that this place exists? You must be or you cannot make the trip to search for it. It will be a difficult and dangerous climb and you will need Spirit help to find the cave. Doubters have no place on that mountain."

They want very much to believe. Both of them. I see it in their faces. They are already planning an expedition.

"When are you going?" I ask Johnny.

"As soon as possible. Winter comes early up there," he answers.

I look at him. He grins and shrugs. Of course! He has what he wants. This is what he has wanted all along. He is about to set forth to search for a cave he believes I have described. They all believe I am a prophet of some kind.

I believe it is a mistake, the wrong message. I am not right for the part; it is bad casting. I am a false prophet, an ordinary woman with peculiar dreams. I believe this can only lead to disaster. I did not choose this, or earn it. Besides, look what happens to prophets. They get their heads handed up on a platter. What happens when they cannot find their cave? I was a coward. I got into all this because I was afraid. Wrong motive!

As I look at them, I see that they believe in spite of themselves. They *want* to believe; they *need* to believe. Everyone wants to think they have an edge. There is hope glimmering in their eyes. How long has it been since their race had a hope of real survival?

Well, why not? My world owes them. Maybe I am some kind of atonement. I just hope it does not go sour for them.

In the name of love, all sorts of atrocities have been committed against them. The missionaries thought they were saving their poor heathen souls by destroying their culture and ending their benighted "devil" worship. Am I to be a reverse missionary? Is that as deluded? It certainly is as confused. Am I to roll back the carpet of plastic turf and let the natural grasses come back, grasses whose seeds are always there, waiting? Am I to lead these people back to the wilderness they were led out of? The wind shall smell of the earth again and not of burning plastic. Heaven help us all.

Let them have their cave, their refuge. Let them have some pride and some purpose. Even if the white man should rethink his violent ways and not destroy himself, let the Native American have some of his own back. Let him believe that he can survive and redeem a destroyed world. It will help him feel like more than an oppressed victim. It can do no more harm than has been already done. Let the hunt for the cave begin.

TWENTY

Johnny is busy with preparations for the expedition. It is getting late and there is not much time before the snow. I finally corner him. "What about me? What do I do now?"

"You're a big girl now. You'll have to make up your own mind. You could come with us if you wanted. You've toughened up a lot."

I could live up to his expectations, live out his dream. Like poor Darlene. Did he make a speech like that to her, too. I would imagine he gave her less option. I do not dare say these things aloud. There are things you learn not to say when you have been part of a man–woman partnership as long as I have. You hold back because the words will do too much damage, hurt more than you intend.

I do not need to say anything. The damage is already done. Darlene has come between us, marring my image of Johnny. It is something that has to be resolved. I cannot make any kind of decision without it.

"Johnny? I have to talk to you now."

"You can come with me to Alma's. I have to pick up a backpack and a tent from her place."

We walk along the peaceful sidewalk, isolated by the normal summer noises of kids roller-skating and a radio playing rock-and-roll nearby.

"Johnny? Please tell me about Flint. And Darlene? I need to know. It's not just curiosity. It has come up and is lying there between us, an argument waiting to explode at the wrong time."

"There isn't any right time. Shit. I wish I hadn't brought you to Jude's!"

"But you did. I think you wanted her to tell me, so you wouldn't have to. Why does it hurt so much?"

"Because I was wrong! I misjudged. I didn't understand and I hurt Darlene beyond her capacity to tolerate. I lost her respect and her love, and I deserved to. No human being has the right to break another's spirit. Is that what you wanted to know? I'm not perfect. I make mistakes. Bad ones. And I pay for them. I don't take it well. OK? Anything else?"

I feel miserable. I wanted him to make that feeling go away but it has only gotten worse. It lies between us like his anger and his hurt, which are naked now, indecently uncovered.

I search for words, hoping to drain his wound, not widen it. "If you had understood, had known, you would have handled it better. You wouldn't have insisted she stay."

"I didn't insist! Dammit. She didn't *resist*!"

"I thought modern young Native American women were more militant feminists."

He shrugs. "You saw Jude. And the others. There are a few who demand their rights. They're listened to politely, today. But they learn it's like spitting into the wind. You get it all over yourself. In the end most of them give up in the interest of being an Indian first. The Indian male ego has been so badly bruised it requires intensive care. Some of the girls go off with white men and are just as miserable as their white sisters. Out here, equality for women means the right to work your tail off supporting your kids and your old man."

"Darlene didn't tell you how she felt?"

"She didn't have the courage. She was so damned young! She just bowed her head and took it. It was my fault. I was all swagger and drive and enthusiasm. I rode over her misery. I should have seen that she couldn't protest, I should have understood how she felt! You'd have flat out said 'no' if you felt that strongly, wouldn't you?"

"I'd at least have made you miserable enough to realize something was wrong, yes. But passive resistance is an insidious disease. You should know that. It's part of your oppressed Indian heritage. It takes a lot of cultural encouragement to learn how to say 'no' when you've been taught all your life to endure in silence."

He picks up a rubber ball lying on the sidewalk and hurls it savagely against the door of the nearest garage. It sails back over our heads and across the street. His voice is strained. "At first I considered chucking the camp and the whole concept. But I couldn't. There was more at stake than my own comfort, my happiness. I was convinced I was going to discover something important there. And I did. Or you did. Darlene was not the cedar tree. And if I had been happily married to her, I would never have brought you home with me. It was meant to happen."

"I hope it justifies your faith!"

I realize that I have found a new dedication, a new personal reason for wanting it all to end well. Darlene and Flint have suffered for this. Their pain should not be wasted. It will be all right. It is better now. I will give Flint an extra hug. And there's one more thing I can do, that I *want* to do for Flint. And for Johnny. He has given me so much. He has helped me heal my wounds; now I want to help him heal his. But how?

I feel I know him so much better now. He's held me when I needed his caring and support, but holding him will not help; he needs more. Poor Johnny has isolated himself in his quest and in his pain and he can't get down off that rock alone. What was it I said to him?... That he needed a god to carry him off on its back? Spirit help. I even promised I would try to arrange it. I was not serious, but what if I could make good on that promise? I can try.

Perhaps once again, with help from the spirits, his spirits who have become mine, I can reach deep enough inside myself with love. . . . and . . . I have it. It has been there all along.

I reach out and touch Johnny's arm. He flinches. My dear Johnny!

"Johnny, please. Listen to me. Remember when I told you that the boy on Pinnacle Rock couldn't save himself because he was challenging the gods? He had so much pride he thought he could be more than human. You are right; you have a lot in common with that boy. You expect yourself to be perfect, to not make mistakes like other humans do. But you are human. You did make a mistake, and you've been punishing yourself ever since.

"I don't think your aunt would expect you to be a god; why do you expect it of yourself?! You weren't all wrong; a lot of what you did was right. But you expected as much of Darlene as you expected of yourself, and that wasn't possible. It's okay to be human, Johnny. If you make a mistake, you just have to make it right."

"And how am I supposed to do that?!!" His tone cuts like a knife.

"With Flint, the innocent victim in all this."

"What more can I do? I already give Jude money."

"You can love him. Be a good father to him."

"But I can't bear to look at the kid, dammit; it hurts so much!"

"You could if you could forgive yourself. You can do heroic things down here just as well. Climb down off that rock. Join the rest of us mortals."

Johnny is frowning but he is listening. "But how?!! How do I do that?!!"

"I think you ask for help. You admit you don't have all the answers. The spirits will help you, if you'll let them. They helped me. You told me to trust them; take your own advice! I may not turn out to be the prophet you want to believe I am. You may not find the cave, but I *am* right about this, and you know I am."

I have done all that I can do for him. I have reached him. It's up to him now. And I have made a decision. It is Johnny's quest, and his tribe's. There is no part in it for me. I cannot let him take me past my depth. And he accepts that. It is a leave taking and we both know it. I will miss him terribly.

"Johnny? I know the time is short, but could we go back to your camp for a few days?"

He nods, reluctantly. He is eager to get started on his trip but he feels he must repay this debt to me. I have helped his people.

The ride back to camp is made in silence, both of us busy in our private worlds. I am testing my new balance. I have learned to walk without my crutch. I must stand alone now, fully free. It is my rebirth and it has, as all rebirths have, a small death in it. I have lost Johnny. But he never truly belonged to me.

Johnny's camp is unbearably dear to me. I see it through fresh, young eyes. I have moved through my life in a half-light, seeing only reflections of all that I am now permitted to see directly. I shield my eyes from the sharp-edged clearness of light and shadow. Miracles of creation lay exposed by each retreating tide.

Man cannot fly, but winged creatures can. My wings are fully dried and strong. I soar, up into the thinning air, through the soft morning, my colors blending with the rainbow mist. I am invincible. I am one with the universe, master of the thunderheads, creator of the lightning bolt, wielder of all creative force. I am Thunderbird, feathered death, swooping from the sky, scattering legends like raindrops on a glassy sea.

Johnny watches me, laughing and then pensive. Summer has ripened and fallen to the ground to spill its seed. The vine maples have reddened and the skies turn dark with morning fogs.

Johnny packs me up one morning.

"Summer's over," he says with awful finality. "Winter will be here too soon. This camp is miserable in the winter."

"And you have a cave to find, and I have a new life to build."

I get back on the motorcycle.

I cling to his back, my hot tears soaking his shirt. But I cannot protest. Not even when he drops me at a stoplight in downtown Seattle.

"Johnny? I hope you find what you're looking for."

He grins, "Dream chasers are never satisfied. You're a helluva woman, in case I never told you."

I cannot see him for the tears. When I have wiped them away, he is gone.

Was he ever really there? He had the quality of a dream, the whole summer did. I look down at my worn blue jeans, stiff with dirt, and my bare feet, and laugh. The last time those feet were on Seattle streets they were in hose and very uncomfortable but terribly chic high heels. And they always had a destination.

I study my image in the store window. An unfamiliar face stares back, young, solemn, wide-eyed, with tear-stained cheeks; thin, vital, and strong. This stranger is going to take some getting used to. She laughs mockingly, contagiously back at me. She looks like someone I might enjoy getting to know.

EPILOGUE

The Boy Who Rode Sharks spread his elk skin robe on the sand for the Corn Maiden. As the moon finished its journey, they labored at their breeding, sowing seeds as numberless as the grains of sand beneath their robe. Their lustful cries woke the sleeping gulls and nesting mallards nearby, who echoed them. Whenever The Boy Who Rode Sharks would fall down exhausted, the woman would raise him, encouraging, enticing, urgent and insatiable. She gave him no peace, demanding, lusting after his seed.

The Boy Who Rode Sharks labored until the sky grew pale with the birth of the sun. With the first rays of the new day, he sank back upon the sand, all life drained from him. As the sun grew hotter, the woman's belly swelled and ripened and then split open scattering millions of seeds onto the sand. Then she joined the Boy Who Rode Sharks in the Spirit World.

Corn Maiden went to the Spirit, Changing Woman.

"I have done what was asked of me," she said.

Changing Woman was pleased.

"You did well. Now you may stay here or you may choose to go back to earth to finish your time with your own people. If you go back, you may take with you any gift from the Spirit World that you choose."

"I would like to return," Corn Maiden replied, "and I would like to take with me the gift of creating beauty."

Changing Woman smiled and nodded, "It is done."

The seeds generated by Corn Maiden and the Boy Who Rode Sharks sprouted and grew into strange plants with fruit that glowed like the sun. If you saw it, you could not resist tasting it. Changing Woman gathered up the delicious looking fruit and put it under her magic hat. She carried it to the top of the tallest rock along the shore. She spread the finest of the fruit out on the rock in the shape of killer whale, the Thunderbird's favorite food, and then hid inside an eagle's nest on the rock beside the fruit.

When Thunderbird passed by he saw the feast spread out below and swooped down to try it. While he was eating, Changing Woman came out of the nest and climbed onto his back. He did not notice her and kept eating.

When the fruit was gone, Thunderbird flew off toward his hidden cave in the mountains and valleys and forest and rivers. Changing Woman kept dropping pieces of the fruit along the way. Whenever she dropped one, Thunderbird would swoop down to eat it, and Changing Woman would hurry and collect animals, fish, and birds, and people of different tribes that were in that place. She brought them all with her on Thunderbird's back.

After a while the load on his back got heavy. Thunderbird was full of the strange fruit and very tired. He hurried to his secret cave in the mountains and fell asleep. While he slept, Changing Woman and the people and animals got off his back and slipped into his cave and into the green valley of the cave.

When he woke, Thunderbird was angry because Changing Woman had tricked him into showing the people his hidden cave. He raised up a mighty storm with his giant wings. Outside the cave there was destruction, but the people and animals inside stayed safe.

Changing Woman planted the rest of the fruit in the valley of the cave where it grew and produced enough fruit to feed everyone. The people sacrificed some of the fruit to Thunderbird, who forgave them.

Thunderbird was so tamed by the fruit the people fed him, that he protected the people of his cave, so that when the spirits became very angry and threatened the earth outside, his people and animals stayed safe within.

ABOUT THE AUTHOR

Although *Corn Maiden* is her first published work, Joyce Jones has been writing for over fifty years. Born and raised in the Midwest, Joyce graduated from the University of Texas with double majors in English and Psychology, earning her Phi Beta Kappa key.

While raising five children, Joyce taught English at Otterbein College in Ohio. After moving to the Pacific Northwest, she worked as a caseworker for the Washington State Department of Public Assistance, in addition to assisting Native American clients of the Bureau of Indian Health.

In 1974 Joyce set out to break the mold of the romance novel genre, turning her back on the chauvinistic formulas that were so predominantly published. To compose *Corn Maiden*, her first book, she incorporated her knowledge and passion for the Native American culture with her own unique personal experiences and style.

For the last ten years Joyce has been working as a sculptor at a local workshop in Edmonds, Washington. She is at present writing two new books, and she enjoys spending time with her first great-grandson.